I0554094

I HAVE
LIVED

"*I Have Lived* is a remarkable, breathtaking novella filled with romance and suspense that will keep you on the edge of your seat, hoping it will never end—one of the best novellas ever."

—GREGORY M. PACIFIC

Retired school teacher, counselor, supervisor, and scholarship and academic director

"Doug has truly awakened his inner author and placed it on full display with *I Have Lived*! Punching well above its weight class, his novella draws you in as it weaves across continents, combining finely researched details with larger-than-life characters from Africa to Afghanistan, while its main character stays grounded by a love that is as deep as it is strong. Anyone who has been tested—or knows others who have—will find something sweet and meaningful in *I Have Lived*!"

—MIKE DONIGER

Former decorated U.S. Navy Submarine Officer, COO and Founder of Chaberton Energy

"*I Have Lived* presents an exceptional story that carries the reader through one man's journey of discovery, through courage, honor, sacrifice, hope, friendship, and romance, to God's unfailing love. From the close, intimate relationships borne in combat, to the touching bond between divergent souls met in the wilds of Africa, to the love of a special, faith-driven woman, this novella covers all the bases. It is a story about the deepest kind of injuries, and the greatest of all cures: the love of family and friends, and God's amazing grace. The story is compelling, with striking visuals, a unique depth of character, and a firm, unfailing commitment to

Faith. The author has dug deep to create this remarkable novella and I recommend it wholeheartedly."

—DAVE PRATT

Author of the *Home Team* series

Lieutenant Colonel (Retired), U.S. Army

"A compelling and inspirational story of true heroes. Doug Lanzo does an extraordinary job of portraying the dedication, courage, and passion of the post-9-11 American veteran and of the spouses and partners who love them."

—E.G. MATTHEWS

Combat Army Veteran, Afghanistan, and Iraq

"*I Have Lived* is an excellent romance novella that keeps the pages turning with effective use of flashbacks. Extremely well written and well researched, I felt like I received a genuine insider peek into the sacrifices and brotherhood of armed forces as well as the culture and traditions of the Maasai people. I would highly recommend this book."

—DARWIN OLYMPIA

Managing Director, Shields & Company

"A captivating blend of human behavior and spirituality. Merits not just one, but multiple readings. I enjoyed *The Year of the Bear* but Mr. Lanzo outdid himself with this novella.The epilogue was beautiful . . . I had to stop and take a moment to worship."

—REBECA CORTEZ

Behavior Analyst and Social Media Influencer

I HAVE LIVED

DOUGLAS J. LANZO

AMBASSADOR INTERNATIONAL
GREENVILLE, SOUTH CAROLINA & BELFAST, NORTHERN IRELAND

www.ambassador-international.com

I HAVE LIVED

©2024 by Douglas J. Lanzo
All rights reserved

ISBN: 978-1-64960-407-1
eISBN: 978-1-64960-455-2

Cover Design by Hannah Linder Designs
Interior Typesetting by Dentelle Design
Edited by Sarah Johnson

Scripture quotations are from the ESV® Bible (The Holy Bible, English Standard Version®), © 2001 by Crossway, a publishing ministry of Good News Publishers. Used by permission. All rights reserved. The ESV text may not be quoted in any publication made available to the public by a Creative Commons license. The ESV may not be translated in whole or in part into any other language.

No part of this publication may be reproduced, distributed, or transmitted in any form or by any means, including photocopying, recording, or other electronic or mechanical methods, without the prior written permission of the publisher, except in the case of brief quotations embodied in critical reviews and certain other noncommercial uses permitted by copyright law. For permission requests, contact the publisher using the information below.

This is a work of fiction. Names, characters, and incidents are all products of the author's imagination or are used for fictional purposes. Any resemblance to actual events or persons, living or dead, is entirely coincidental. Any mentioned brand names, places, and trademarks remain the property of their respective owners, bear no association with the author or the publisher, and are used for fictional purposes only.

AMBASSADOR INTERNATIONAL
Emerald House
411 University Ridge, Suite B14
Greenville, SC 29601
United States
www.ambassador-international.com

AMBASSADOR BOOKS
The Mount
2 Woodstock Link
Belfast, BT6 8DD
Northern Ireland, United Kingdom
www.ambassadormedia.co.uk

The colophon is a trademark of Ambassador, a Christian publishing company.

In memory of Peter Alderman, charismatic friend and beloved New Yorker who tragically perished in the cowardly 9-11 attacks on the World Trade Center. His life and death inspired an entire foundation named in his honor and the generations succeeding him to carry on his heroic legacy of healing survivors of terror attacks and mass violence around the globe from trauma and other emotional wounds. It also inspired me to write the following poem in his honor on the twentieth anniversary of 9-11:

Twenty Years of Pain: Remembering 9-11

By Douglas J. Lanzo

Twenty years since it happened,

yet it seems like yesterday,

that two planes pierced twin towers,

shattering all one dark day.

A time still raw remembered

when close friend laid down his life,

atop Windows on the World,

his last breaths cutting like a knife.

Did he plummet through the air,

watching his fate close to ground,

or endure the raging heat,

as smoke and fire did surround?!?

No words can heal the sorrow,

or absorb the grievous pain —

wounds too deep for time to salve,

echoed by each passing rain.

Why God ordained us to live

begs of purpose we must find

worthy of those perished souls . . .

whose memories were refined.

AUTHOR'S NOTE

Have Lived is a gripping, romantic, suspense novella that tells the remarkable life story of Lieutenant Brian Johnson, a former Army Ranger medic, and his bride, Beth McKenzie, through a series of flashbacks to defining moments of their lives on their wedding day. Far from a traditional romance, at its core lie compelling accounts of events that transformed Brian and Beth into men and women of uncommon valor, compassion, faith, and honor. Thrust into extreme dangers, confronted by suffering, and buffeted by twists of fate, their principles are put to extreme tests which forge their character before our very eyes. From the ghettoes of apartheid-era Soweto to the mountaintop battlefields of Afghanistan, we are swept across the globe with them, sharing their triumphs and tragedies in riveting scenes that touch our hearts, challenge our minds, and inspire our souls.

Deeply impacted by the tragic events and unspeakable evils that unfolded on 9-11, I experienced firsthand the loss of a close friend and much beloved New Yorker, Peter Alderman. Peter was forced to make the most harrowing of decisions on that dark day. Through the most bitter of circumstances, he found himself trapped atop Windows on the World on the 106th floor of the World Trade Center, where he was helping to deliver a Bloomberg presentation. Below him raged an inferno forged from evil and hate from which there was no way to save his youthful life. Much to their tribute, his family established a foundation in his name and honor to benefit those suffering from terrorism, poverty, and mental health issues around the world. His inspirational life and the equally inspiring work of the Peter C. Alderman Foundation were a significant motivation for me to write *I Have Lived*.

I also drew inspiration from *The Hunt For Bin Laden* by Robin Moore, a truly engaging and fascinating account of the courageous and mission-driven members of our Special Forces, who, despite their limited numbers, successfully partnered with the Northern Alliance to free Afghanistan from the harsh grip of Taliban rule. The harrowing battles they endured in forcing Osama Bin Laden and the Taliban leaders to flee the terrorist sanctuary inspired the gritty battlefield scenes of *I Have Lived*. The careful research for these battle scenes paid off, culminating with a retired Special Forces colonel characterizing them as well-written and realistic.

The character of Lieutenant Brian Johnson was inspired by real-life, American heroes like Pat Tillman, the Arizona Cardinal and College Hall of Fame safety who turned down a multi-million-dollar NFL offer to re-sign in order to serve his country in Afghanistan as an Army Ranger. Researching the heroic role of the Army Rangers throughout our nation's distinguished miliary history, I was incredibly humbled to learn of their mission to engage enemy forces at close quarters in critical, direct-fire battles.

From helping to earn our nation's freedom as famed riflemen during the Revolutionary War, to fighting in key battles to free North Africa from Nazi control, to storming the beaches of Normandy on

D-Day during World War II, the Rangers established themselves as the premier light infantry of the army and duly earned the motto, "Rangers, lead the way!" Thus, it was a natural decision that protagonist Lieutenant Brian Johnson, a man of honor and sacrifice, would be a medical officer within that most heralded of designations in the U.S. Army—the Army Rangers.

The medical profiles of both Brian, a U.S. Ranger medic; his bride, Beth, a registered nurse; and the medical doctors, nurses, paramedics, and missionaries featured in the novella draw inspiration from friends, family members, and other medical heroes whose sacrifice, compassion, wisdom, and talents have forged in me a deep admiration, respect, and gratitude for who they are and what they do tirelessly on a daily basis to improve our lives and the lives of those struggling with medical needs around the globe. The medical mission trips of Black Rock Congregational Church that my mother helped to organize and that my brother led to treat and minister to children and teens suffering from HIV in the ghettoes of South Africa particularly informed my decision to feature African medical mission trips in *I Have Lived*.

I hold a similar admiration for the goodness and generosity of the Maasai people, a simple but noble, pastoral tribe of red-robed cattle and goatherders whom you may know as traditionally sending their teenage boys armed only with spears to slay full-grown lions in order to come of age as tribal warriors. Despite that fierce rite of passage, this tribe has an incredibly endearing heart. The Maasai people stunned the world by presenting America with their most sacred gift following 9-11, a sacrificial offering that you will learn more about in the pages to come. The noble and generous members of the Maasai tribe prove captivating characters in the novella, with one of their young warriors playing a strong supporting role. As they brighten the lives of Brian and Beth, they, too, in turn, are touched by the godly ministries of health and goodwill offered by the couple and their families.

Without giving away the particulars, you will recognize other heroes within the novella: inspirational figures in sports, the military, medical philanthropy, and politics. However, I sincerely hope and believe that you will find that the most true-to-life and inspirational figures are the ones you learn of for the first time in reading this novella. As their wedding day unfolds in quite unexpected ways, you will experience firsthand the trials and tribulations that forge Brian and Beth into the principled and resilient Christian couple you find that day at the altar.

Set in 2004, the main inspiration for the timing of releasing *I Have Lived* has been to uplift readers with a powerful example of meaningful living during these increasingly unsettling post-pandemic times.

Readers who enjoy a riveting story packed with realistic combat and moving scenes of exemplary love, sacrifice, service, and honor will be drawn to the inner peace and strength exuded by the main characters amidst great tumults. It is my sincere hope and prayer that *I Have Lived* immerses you in a refreshing and exhilarating journey.

DOUGLAS J. LANZO

CHAPTER 1

An attractive, sunburned, twelve-year-old girl sat upon a small hill overlooking a vast savannah. Below her, an intense heat radiated through sprawling grasslands dotted with flat-topped acacia, yellow-green patches of sparse forest and brush, and a few rivers winding their way with life-giving waters. The sight before her liquid brown eyes was spectacular, causing her to gape in awe at the beauty and abundance of the wildlife roaming the Maasai Mara Game Reserve.

Fittingly, the girl with soft features thought, *this is considered by many to be not only the greatest game reserve in Kenya—or even in Africa—but also the greatest one on earth.*

While herds of gazelles, zebras, antelopes, and gnus grazed tranquilly, a herd of wildebeests leaped into a mighty, mud-brown river—fording crocodile-infested waters—and thundered across the vista. Her eardrums reverberated with the sounds of their hooves trampling the underbrush as they lunged from the river, creating cascading waves of dust. She was relieved by the sounds of their snorts as they dodged the steely jaws of crocodiles to traverse the river.

"Oh no!" she presently cried out at the sound of a young wildebeest's moan as a crocodile wrestled it into the river's muddy depths. Although warned that this would happen by a Maasai village guide the day before, it jarred her, nonetheless.

The guide had brought her and her parents to this very spot the day before.

"Do you see that herd?" he had asked them, pointing toward the far edge of the savannah, where she had beheld a vast but distant herd of wildebeests. "And that fist in the sky?"

Shielding her eyes from the yet strong sun, she had noted dark storm clouds gathering above the horizon.

"It clenches with life-giving rain," he had explained with flashing eyes. "The herd will follow it across a river of death in order to live. The Mara River gives life and takes it away. It is full of crocodiles, hiding in its angry waters. They wait each summer for the wildebeests to cross."

Startled by sudden movement in the thickets at the edge of the hill, the girl's focus abruptly shifted. Though straining somewhat to do so, she could make out the figure of a cheetah slinking stealthily through the underbrush toward the fringes of a gazelle herd. As she knew from the village guide, although cheetahs had great speed, they could only sustain those speeds for short bursts. Thus, they needed to approach close to their prey before giving chase.

Further away, she spotted a mother elephant and her calf foraging for grass and other vegetation along the savannah. Although larger than any other animals in sight, they were considerably smaller than the massive twelve-thousand-pound, solitary bull that she had observed earlier that week dexterously manipulating its trunk to pluck pieces of fruit from a tree.

Spotting movement in the foreground not more than one thousand yards away from her, the mesmerized girl saw a majestic, black-maned lion pace in agitation before warily setting itself down in the grass.

What could be alarming this magnificent creature? Beth wondered.

Peering in the direction of the lion's gaze, she saw the brilliant red robe of a Maasai *moran* illuminated by the fiery rays of the late afternoon sun. Instinctively, the lions of the reserve associated the red-robed figure with danger. As Beth knew, the nomadic Maasai tribe killed lions both to protect their prized cattle and to test their young warriors. Indeed, as part of a centuries-old tradition to prove their manhood, to that date the young Maasai *morani* were required to venture into the savannah alone—armed only with a spear—to confront and slay a lion.

Not appreciating the reason for the lion's agitation, the girl remained puzzled. She soon noticed, however, that not far behind the Maasai *moran* was a young, Caucasian boy. Each of them silently approached her perch, armed only with a spear and a club. As soon as they drew close enough for her to recognize the boy, Beth stood up and called out excitedly, "Brian! Brian!"

The slender girl's sudden movement and shouting caused quite a stir among the wildlife. Counterintuitive to Beth's expectations, gazelles in the closest herd warily approached her, assessing whether or not she posed a danger to them. As she began to run toward Brian and his Maasai companion, some gazelles displayed an even more surprising behavior, bouncing up and down on their four legs in a display of alarm. Having at last concluded that the youth was not headed in their direction and no longer posed an immediate threat, the gazelles ceased their pronking. However, they maintained a vigilant eye on the stranger.

Meanwhile, the prowling cheetah quietly receded into some thickets closer to the edge of the forest. The black-maned lion, likewise agitated by the girl and the commotion, rose to his feet and moved at a steady trot across the savannah, prompting herds of zebras, antelopes, and gazelles to edge away from the noble beast.

Brian presently waved to the girl as she approached and called out her name.

Beth had arrived ten days earlier to the Maasai village adjoining Maasai Mara Game Reserve as part of a medical mission team sponsored by her church in Arlington, Virginia. The team included her father—an orthopedic surgeon—two primary care physicians, two registered nurses, Beth, and four other church members without medical training who came to assist the team in any way possible as supervised laypersons. They saw the medical mission as a unique opportunity to demonstrate Christian love and compassion in ministering to the most basic physical needs of a noble but primitive tribe, which had resisted change for centuries.

Primarily known in the West for their warrior spirit, the Maasai people, as Beth's father had taught her, traditionally clung fiercely to their cultural traditions and rejected foreign influences. Most of the Maasai lived in thatched huts, or *bomas*, and lacked running water, electricity, telephones, and most other vestiges of modern civilization. From the beginning of their history, these proud nomads had raised cattle as their source of livelihood; relying on them for food, milk, clothing, and shelter.

In addition, many Maasai continued to maintain an age-old belief that their god had directly given their ancestors cattle from Heaven. In fact, convinced that during the course of history, neighboring peoples had stolen their god-given cattle, the Maasai had *retrieved* cattle from them over the years. This had, unsurprisingly, provoked periodic inter-tribal conflict.

Thus, cattle were considered precious and cherished above all of their other possessions. Maasai *morani* considered it a sacred duty to frequently risk their lives in battle to protect cattle from lions, leopards, and other predators.

Knowing this, the actions of the Maasai people in the wake of September 11 had deeply moved Beth, her father, Sheldon, and the rest of their former mission team nearly a decade after their trip. The Maasai people had donated fourteen of their life-giving cows to American diplomats in order to help the victims of the attacks. Despite barely understanding what a skyscraper was, the Maasai people had listened intently as a Maasai elder, returning to his people from New York following that dark day, described in the simplest of terms the wrenching loss of life and horrific destruction. The elder explained, with animated words and gestures, the deadly flames caused by the suicide planes at the Pentagon and the horrifying collapse of the World Trade Center's twin towers. The Maasai people were stunned and heartbroken by the account of the devastating attack.

Their sacrificial reaction to the news was hailed around the world as the "ultimate gift," an act of love and generosity which demonstrated, in the words of that Maasai elder, that his people were "merciful" and, though "fierce and deadly when provoked," could "easily cry for the pain of other people."

"Their gift epitomized the love of Christ, despite their ignorance of His atoning love for them. That is why we were there—to share through our medical ministry the Good News with this good-hearted people," Beth's dad had recounted years later in passing the baton to a new generation of medical ambassadors inspired by the compassion of the Maasai people.

"This is Kimeli," Brian said, introducing his Maasai friend to Beth. "He's been showing me the wildlife around here up close."

Beth smiled and held out her hand. "Pleased to meet you, Kimeli. My name is Beth."

"*Yeyo, takwenya!*" Kimeli said in the traditional Maasai greeting to women. "It is great to meet you, Beth," he said in British-accented English. "And you may respond, if you like, *Iko!*"

"Iko!" Beth repeated with a pleasant giggle.

Standing before her was a tall, lithe boy who had recently become a warrior by successfully undergoing a painful circumcision ritual before his entire village without flinching. Clad in a vibrant red robe and decorated with orange warrior paint, Kimeli cast a strikingly handsome figure.

As he spoke, Beth noticed his lack of lower front teeth. At a young age, two of Kimeli's tooth buds had been purposely removed in order to enable him to whistle more effectively to the cattle that the village *morani* herded and protected. Beth was also immediately struck by Kimeli's elaborately braided hair and colorful necklaces, two of which crisscrossed his chest and disappeared under his robe.

"I love your beaded necklaces," Beth said in genuine admiration.

"Thank you, Beth. God blessed you with a beautiful face," Kimeli replied, causing Beth to blush.

Kimeli's reference to God was all the more remarkable because he was referring to a Christian God. In a rare occurrence among the Maasai people, Brian's father, Stephen, had led Kimeli and his father to Christ after several months of biblical teachings and discussions coupled with charitable work for the benefit of the Maasai villagers.

Stephen was a Baptist missionary who had been living among the Maasai people in a *boma* for a ten-month period beginning last September. Brian and his mother, Catherine, had joined him five weeks earlier in June once Brian had completed his seventh-grade classes back in Havre de Grace, Maryland. Arriving at a Maasai village just north of the Maasai Mara Game Reserve on September 1, 1992, Stephen had found that the Maasai adhered to centuries-old customs and traditions, including male circumcision, polygamy, and the sacrosanct passage of a male from boy to warrior to elder.

With respect to religion, the Maasai did not have clearly defined spiritual beliefs, although they prayed to a god, or *engai*, whom they believed to be an invisible force governing the universe. Though kind and generous to Stephen, the Maasai quickly made clear to the missionary that they took immense pride in their culture, viewed their religious philosophy as an integral part of their culture, and had no intention of re-evaluating it anytime in the foreseeable future.

The aftermath of a discussion of the Holocaust one October evening changed everything. When Stephen informed the Maasai elders of the Nazi's slaughter of innocent Jewish men, women, and children and attempted extermination of an entire people based on their ethnic heritage, the Maasai exhibited great concern, asking Stephen what evil force could bring this about. The elders began to question each other about the morality of former acts of their people and neighboring tribes, including the nineteenth century Maasai dispute over livestock and grazing rights that had culminated in members of the Laikipia Tribe being taken to a crater and hurled to their deaths. This precipitated a discussion of the nature of man, free will, and sin.

Soon, Stephen found himself illustrating the fundamental principles of Christianity using the colorful beads of the Maasai people. A black bead represented sin, a red bead for Jesus' blood and forgiveness of sins, a green bead meaning new life in Christ, a white bead representing the Holy Spirit, a yellow bead signifying God's light and glory, a blue bead characterizing baptism, a purple bead denoting the crown of everlasting life, and a gold bead symbolizing Heaven. This, and the metaphor of the metamorphosis of a caterpillar into a butterfly, conveyed in a concrete and readily understandable format the principal truths of the Christian faith to a number of the Maasai elders who, in turn, imparted them to their wives and children, including Kimeli.

"We have a dance at our village this evening," Kimeli said. "You and Brian are welcome. One of our *morani* is getting married. It will be a great celebration."

A Maasai wedding involved festivities and dancing in which the entire village participated, but foreigners were rarely invited to attend. By extending this invitation, Kimeli was signaling to Brian and Beth that he considered them to be part of the Maasai community.

"That sounds wonderful," Beth responded.

"We would love to go to the wedding with you, Kimeli! That sounds like good fun," Brian added.

"Very good. Now, I must join the other *morani* at the *manyatta*," Kimeli stated, referring to a segregated community in which all of the *morani* lived during the warrior stage of their progression to full manhood. "Please come to the fire by the village center after the sun sets. That is where we will be dancing."

"No problem, Kimeli. We're excited to go. It'll be a big honor for us," Brian said solemnly, as Kimeli nodded and took his leave. Brian knew that once Kimeli had completed his rite of passage into full manhood, he would be an esteemed elder of his people for the rest of his life.

"He seems like such a gracious and friendly person," Beth told Brian.

"Yes, he's a great friend, one of the nicest guys in the entire village," Brian answered.

"I will miss him when I leave this week," Beth said. "And I will especially miss you. I will never forget you," Beth continued, looking into Brian's eyes.

Brian gently clasped Beth's hand, and together, they looked out onto the most beautiful sunset they had ever seen.

CHAPTER 2

The day before her medical mission trip was to end, Beth sat atop a hill overlooking a vast savannah forged from ancient times. Once a volcano that shaped the wombs for dinosaurs to roam the Great Rift Valley, the hill was now harmlessly dotted with acacia trees and sun-drenched grasses of varying yellow and green hues. Gazing down its gentle slopes, the girl beheld a verdant oasis teaming with exotic life.

She observed the lyre-shaped horns of a herd of gazelles as they tranquilly grazed upon awakening grasslands. Peering a bit further into the tree-dotted savannah, she noted the cantering of a herd of zebras casting guileful illusions upon her eyes. One moment, the zebras appeared to individually exude their natural patterns of black and white, while in the next moment, the shifting herd appeared to meld magically into a single shade of gray. The herd followed blue-sheened wildebeest as they trotted to new foraging ground upon the grasslands.

Presently, a handsome figure clad in a red tunic made his measured way up the slope toward her. She did not observe the figure until a tall boy with light brown hair and sea-blue eyes waved, capturing a tinge of orange sunlight upon his hand in the process.

"Brian!" she shouted, waving to the boy, whose ruddy face instantly smiled back. He scrambled up the top half of the hill, navigating his way through some sickle brush buzzing with bees. Beth could make out that he carried some round, yellow and purple objects in his hands.

"Hey, Beth!" he called out. "I came across a Jackalberry tree on the way and thought you might like them since you like the taste of lemon."

"Oh, Jackalberry fruit, lovely!" Beth replied. "I've never seen a purple one before."

"Usually, the jackals and antelope eat them while they are still yellow, but they turn purple when they are fully ripe. Please try one," he said, handing her a round purple fruit about one inch in diameter.

Biting into it, she found that it tasted both sweet and sour at the same time, evincing a welcome lemony flavor. "It's delicious," she said with a smile.

"I had to make sure you tried it before your trip back home."

"Definitely," Beth said, with a slight sigh of disappointment as the reality of her impending departure sunk in. "I've had such an incredible time here . . . I wish I could stay longer."

"So do I," said Brian, blushing a bit. "Kimeli asked me to bring this to you." Reaching into his tunic, he took out a bright, beaded bracelet of blue, green, yellow, and white colors woven into pyramidal patterns. "He said he hopes to see you later today; but he must participate in a hunt, and he is not certain he will be able to return before you leave."

"Why, it is so beautiful!" Beth exclaimed. "Please thank him from the bottom of my heart."

"I will," Brian promised. "He also said that he hopes one day to be able to visit both of us in America."

"Of course, we will . . . I will, and I'm sure you will . . . I mean, you and I both will one day invite him to visit us in America," Beth said, unsure how to phrase things but hoping in her heart it might be a mutual invitation.

"Yes, we must return the favor. He is a great friend and was so kind to invite us to a Maasai wedding. And I . . . wanted to give you this," Brian said, revealing a leather bag hidden underneath his tunic. Opening the attractive leather bag, embellished with tiny glass beads, Brian displayed an intricately woven, circular necklace of blue, red, yellow, orange, white, and green beads, thirty beads thick. The circular center accented by brilliant triangles reminded Beth of a sun shining in stunning radiance.

"It's gorgeous!" Beth cried out.

"It's a traditional Maasai wedding necklace."

"Wow, it's so spectacular. Brian, this is too much," Beth protested, "It must have cost a fortune, and I'm not sure I deserve it. I mean, it's so beautiful . . . "

"As the kindest and most beautiful person I have ever met, you deserve it," Brian stated with conviction.

"Oh, Brian," Beth said, tearing up.

"I don't know whether I'll ever see you again. But the necklace symbolizes how I feel about you, and it's a promise that I will never forget you, no matter what happens."

"I hope we will get to see each other in America," Beth said, embracing Brian. "I couldn't imagine things any other way."

CHAPTER 3

TEN YEARS LATER

An unearthly light, vibrant with color and life, cast itself upon the windswept waters of the Susquehanna River. A small sailboat abruptly tacked as the wind shifted direction, gusting toward the parkland shore. Further away, a double-breasted cormorant battled the wind before disappearing into a burst of sunlight. As Brian peered into the May sunrise, the cormorant reemerged as if ablaze, bearing the glorious, fiery orange illumination of another world.

An ordinary bird transformed by the radiance of the heavens, Brian mused, reflecting on the spectacular hue and the seabird's heralding the arrival of this long-anticipated day. Smiling, the young man rose in a slow but deliberate manner from a time-worn park bench and flexed his shoulders. The funnel of sunlight that presently streamed through the shifting cloud cover onto the handsome body of the twenty-four-year-old energized and rejuvenated him.

It is time, he thought, turning toward the quaint buildings and shops that formed the heart of the Maryland city.

As Brian made his way through the historic city center, he passed a statue of the Marquis de Lafayette, the French Revolutionary War general who fondly named the then-town Havre de Grace after a

French seaport. Translated as Harbor of Mercy, the historic town had been burned by British soldiers in 1777 and bombarded by their navy during the War of 1812. Brian was proud to be a resident of this scenic and historic city, which had, by the narrowest of margins, missed being voted as the nation's capital. In particular, he admired the patriotism of Second Lieutenant John O'Neil, who alone had stood his ground and engaged British troops during the War of 1812 after the local militia retreated. Located at the strategic point where the Susquehanna flows into the Chesapeake Bay, Havre de Grace had served as a frequent crossing point for George Washington during the Revolutionary War.

It's fitting that Washington's soldiers encamped in this city of patriots en route to their historic victory over the British at Yorktown, Brian mused.

It was with excitement, expectancy, and a bit of trepidation that Brian presently opened the door of Java by the Bay to meet his closest friend—a man whom he had not seen for over a year. The penetrating, gray eyes of a solidly built, clean-cut soldier locked on Brian from across the restaurant.

Brian beamed as he approached his fellow Ranger and platoon leader, a man with whom he had served as a Ranger medic in Operation Enduring Freedom in the rugged mountains of Afghanistan.

Before they could even embrace, John crisply brought his right hand to a salute and said, "I salute you as a friend and a hero."

Maintaining his composure with a smile and disavowing shake of his head, the athletic young man warmly embraced his "blood brother."

"It's awesome to see you, John."

"I wouldn't miss this day for the world, buddy. And it's great to see you back on your feet and looking like yourself again."

They each took a seat and ordered a cup of coffee and a bagel. Looking across the table, Brian took a moment to take stock of the man for whom he had fought and risked his life. His mind flashed back to a terrifying day: the last time he had seen First Lieutenant Morrison or anyone else from his platoon.

"It's a hot LZ!" the crew chief shouted to the helicopter pilot as machine-gun fire tore through the nose of the MH-47E Chinook. "Lift, lift, lift!"

The pilot immediately arrested their descent toward the landing zone, pointed the nose of the chopper upward, and began a steep ascent. Brian could see the muzzles of machine-guns from the rocky mountain terrain below as Al-Qaida forces furiously attempted not only to prevent the Ranger reinforcements from landing but also to bring them down. Ominously, the Al-Qaida forces wielded heavier firepower than these machine-guns, including rocket-propelled grenades (RPGs) and shoulder-fired, surface-to-air missiles. They had already brought down an Apache AH-64 helicopter and were closing in on the downed Rangers on the ridgeline below. Having hit the reinforcing Chinook with machine-gun fire, they were chomping at the bit at the prospect of neutralizing the Americans' aerial advantage and bringing the battle to the mountain where the infidels would be destroyed, Allah willing.

The right-door gunner mercilessly poured out machine-gun fire over the kill zone as the Chinook gained altitude. Without warning, an RPG round violently slammed into the chopper, rupturing its hydraulic lines. Brian and the other ten men aboard could feel the chopper shake and then lurch to the side as the pilot desperately strove to keep the chopper stable so they could complete their ascent and find an alternate landing zone. But the loss of hydraulic fluid was serious, risking complete failure of the hydraulic system and causing the controls to respond only intermittently to the frenetic efforts of the pilot. They had no choice but to bring the chopper down in the middle of the kill zone.

"Brace yourselves! We're taking her down!" the co-pilot shouted.

The machine-gun fire intensified as the chopper rapidly descended from three hundred feet, to two hundred feet, and then one hundred feet above the LZ. Several bullets pierced through the helicopter and ricocheted around its interior. Before Brian could assess whether or not the bullets had found their targets, the helicopter landed with a jarring jolt on the rocky terrain, and fellow soldiers began hurriedly exiting the chopper.

"Move out, move out!" Ranger platoon leader John Morrison commanded as his men rushed out of what was now a stationary target. "Take cover! Enemy bunker at ten o'clock! Objective four hundred meters west of enemy position!"

As everyone but one pilot disembarked, the Quick Reaction Force concentrated their machine gun and M-4 rifle fire in the direction of a snowy ridge less than a quarter mile away from which enemy fire rained down upon them. Brian exited the chopper, clutching his nine-millimeter pistol while keeping his profile as low to the ground as possible. His breath crystallized in the thin, cold mountain air as he dove behind a man-sized boulder.

Brian's lungs burned from the exertion of bearing ninety pounds of equipment, ammunition, and medical supplies at this almost two-mile-high elevation. Though stationed in Afghanistan since October, this was by far the highest altitude from which he had fought. He discarded his rucksack behind the cover of the boulder and awaited word of the plan of assault.

As a Ranger combat medic, Brian was trained to wage combat like any other Ranger until a man went down—and he had killed his share of Taliban and Al-Qaida forces over the course of the past few months. He had *also treated wounded comrades: extracting bullets, treating burns, and even amputating limbs. He had operated on fellow Rangers, who had sustained injuries to vital organs—men who had gasped their last breath while his hands strove against all hope to preserve their lives.*

Though such experiences led some to call men like Brian "battle-hardened" and "war-tested," they never became routine or ceased to take their toll on those skilled and fortunate enough to survive them. On the contrary, Brian's dreams were sometimes haunted by images of fallen warriors—men with whom he had trained, fought, and shared a sacred bond—suffering and dying before him. In the worst of such nightmares, Brian watched helplessly as a "blood brother" died before his eyes.

What sustained Brian's spirit in these circumstances, where some only saw the futility of war, were his faith in God; his love for his brethren in arms; the memory of his grandfather; and above all, his conviction that what he was fighting for was good and right. Brian saw Operation Enduring Freedom in much the same way as his grandfather had seen Operation Overlord, the Allied invasion of Nazi-occupied Europe that began on D-Day fifty-eight years earlier: as a righteous battle of the forces of freedom and justice against evil and oppression.

As a Ranger in Company C of the 2nd Ranger Battalion, Brian's paternal grandfather, Raymond Johnson, had stormed Omaha Beach that fateful day on June 6, 1944, marking the commencement of the Allied liberation of Fortress Europe. Shot in the thigh by a Nazi machine-gunner, the wounded Ranger had literally crawled up the adjoining cliffs to join his company and claim the high ground at Omaha Beach that morning. The men of Company C distinguished themselves as the first Allied forces to occupy the strategic cliffs that day. In doing so, they had saved the lives of an untold number of fellow soldiers on the beaches below, sparing them from German fire.

For the valor he displayed in that action and the wounds he sustained, Raymond Johnson was awarded a Bronze Star and a Purple Heart. At an early age, Brian had learned the high cost of freedom from his beloved grandfather. Thirty-seven of the sixty-eight men in Company C were killed or wounded at Normandy that day—the heaviest casualties of any Ranger unit in the massive Allied landing.

"The cost of freedom was high, but the cost of doing nothing was infinitely higher," his grandfather had told Brian in recounting his World War II service.

As a concrete reminder of the importance of his mission in Afghanistan, Brian carried with him a tiny picture of the craters that had once been the twin towers of the World Trade Center. The president's words following the September 11 attacks were seared in Brian's memory. "I will not forget this wound to our country or those who inflicted it," President Bush had stated. "I will not yield; I will not rest; I will not relent in waging this struggle for the freedom and security for the American people."[1]

The mission of Brian and his team that day was to rescue the downed Ranger crew, secure the area, treat and evacuate the wounded, and exfiltrate every soldier, whether dead or alive, from the area. The countervailing enemy objective was to inflict maximum casualties on the Americans and crush their will, just as Afghans had crushed the will of the Soviet Army and every foreign invader in Afghan history. The crucial difference between Operation Enduring Freedom and these attempted conquests was that the Americans and their coalition partners were fighting alongside the Afghan people to liberate Afghanistan and turn it back over to them, rather than to foreign conquerors.

---

1   President George W. Bush's address to a Joint Session of Congress and the American people at the U.S. Capitol on September 20, 2001.

The Ranger crew had assembled into two, five-man teams: Team Alpha, led by John, the commander of their entire forty-one-man platoon, and Team Bravo, led by Sean, the platoon sergeant. Each team had a leader, a combat medic, a weaponry specialist, a communications specialist, and a helicopter crew member: one being the co-pilot and the other, the crew chief. John had assigned Brian to Team Alpha. Each team had immediately taken cover; probed the enemy with fire; and attempted to assess the enemy's strength, position, and weaponry.

Three or four Al-Qaida fighters were visible in the most forward position, engaging Team Alpha with machine-gun fire from behind a snowy, rock-strewn ridge not more than 350 meters away. Seventy or eighty meters beyond them was a larger concentration of enemy combatants, perhaps eight or ten strong, launching RPGs from what appeared to be well-fortified, dug-in positions along the ridgeline. Hundreds of meters further back, Brian could see tiny figures advancing in spurts from caves and covered positions toward an Apache helicopter, from which the downed crew was returning enemy fire.

The firestorm was fierce, and the downed Apache crew was clearly outnumbered. It was only a matter of time before the Al-Qaida fighters would close their deadly noose.

Enemy fire presently hit two Team Bravo Rangers and shattered into fragments that were absorbed by their ceramic body armor. Stronger than Kevlar, the boron carbide ceramic had prevented the life-threatening AK-47 assault rifle fire from penetrating their abdomens and chests. Brian knew that if he and his brothers survived the day, they would likely owe their lives to these remarkable armored plates. Never again would these soldiers question whether the protection was worth the tradeoff in mobility.

John signaled for Team Bravo to get ready to move to a flanking position on elevated ground just east of Al-Qaida's forward position. Shouting above the din of enemy fire, John next instructed Team Alpha to split up into two sub-teams. Three men, including John and Brian, would launch a grenade at the enemy position and then advance to a rocky outcrop fifty meters closer to the Al-Qaida nest. Meanwhile, a two-man team consisting of a machine gunner and an assistant gunner feeding his M240G would cover their advance and attempt to suppress enemy fire with a withering hail of heavy machine-gun fire.

John signaled for the coordinated engagement to begin, and suddenly, everything became surreal to Brian—as if he were in a slow-motion action film. Jim, the weapons specialist, fired an M203 grenade launcher from his M16A2 5.56mm rifle at the enemy position. The grenade exploded several meters short of the target but flung one of the Al-Qaida fighters into the air. Machine-gun fire from the M240G finished the job, killing the Uzbek before he even fell to the ground.

Meanwhile, John, Brian, and Jim pushed forward as fast as they could—despite the treacherous terrain—toward the outcrop. Brian could hear intense machine-gun fire and see from his peripheral vision fuzzy images of Team Bravo members advancing toward their ordered position. The next thing Brian knew, he was thrown to the ground by the impact of a Chinese-made 30mm RPG exploding fifteen meters behind him. Shrapnel flew through the air and tore through Jim's calf, instantly rendering him immobile. Reduced to an easy target and in acute pain, Jim cried out for immediate assistance. "I'm down! I'm down! Brother, I can't move!"

Turning around toward his fallen comrade, Brian used his hands to brace his weight and rise to his feet. Only then did he notice the blood dripping into the snow from his left forearm, which had been lacerated by *a sharp piece of shrapnel. Brian decided to ignore his wound for now and tend to Jim. The first thing he had to do was to get both of them behind cover beside his medical supply pack, where he could safely treat Jim's wound. Bearing most of Jim's weight, Brian helped Jim to hobble on one leg back toward the boulders from which Team Alpha had launched its attack. Machine-gun fire ripped into the ground not more than three meters away as Brian struggled to support Jim through the last few meters of the rocky, snow-laden terrain.*

Meanwhile, John alone had reached the rocky outcrop constituting the Alpha Team's objective. The RPG explosion had separated John not only from Brian and Jim, but also from his gunners by preventing them from following him there. Sean radioed John that his team was now in its flanking position but had sustained a serious injury. Ben, the helicopter pilot, had been shot in his pelvic area and was bleeding profusely.

"What is his condition?" John demanded.

"Serious. The medic says he'll need to give him blood packs to keep him alive and that he won't hold out more than two, three hours max," Sean radioed back. "Can I request an EVAC?"

"We could request one, but there's no way they're going to send an EVAC chopper into a hot LZ in broad daylight," John answered. "We're first going to have to take out the enemy's forward position and their fortified bunker. And the way things are going, we're going to need close air support for that."

"Want me to call in bombs on the bunker?" Sean asked.

"Yes, see if we can get an F-16 or two to take out the bunker," John commanded. "But prioritize calling in 20mm cannon fire to take out some of the Al-Qaida advancing on the Apache."

"Yes, sir."

Sean's communication specialist, Mike, called headquarters and requested air support as well as the frequencies for communicating with incoming jet fighters.

"We have two F-15s inbound—three minutes to target—for the strafe, and a pair of F-16s coming in nine to ten minutes to take out the bunker," Sean reported to John minutes later.

"Good. Let's try to neutralize the forward position in the meantime. Let me know if Ben's condition becomes critical. I'm hoping we can request an EVAC in thirty minutes."

"Roger that."

Though Team Bravo had a definite kill in addition to Team Alpha's grenade kill, at least four Al-Qaida fighters remained near the ridgeline. As the coalition forces were quickly finding out, the Al-Qaida combatants were masters at camouflage and concealment. It was nearly impossible to get a reliable figure on their strength in any one mountain location.

Realizing that they had no choice but to engage the enemy to the maximum if they were to thwart its objective, Sean ordered his weapon specialist to ready the grenade launcher. In a matter of seconds, Carlos turned off the safety, loaded his M203 grenade launcher, and raised the leaf sight to determine the distance to the enemy target. For maximum accuracy, he then fired from a prone position with devastating effect. Two of the remaining fighters were killed instantly, and the other two were thrown into uncovered positions. Fire from Sean's M240G heavy machine-gun cut them down immediately thereafter, eliminating the enemy from its forward position.

Sean, Carlos, and Mike sprang to their feet and moved to secure the former enemy position. A hastily fired, enemy RPG launched from the bunker, thrusting shrapnel into the air a harmless distance away from the approaching men. Having now secured the enemy's forward position, Team Bravo was within seventy-five meters of the bunker. However, the men realized with extreme frustration that they could approach no further. In addition to lacking the firepower to do so, advancing any closer to the bunker would pose a serious risk of their being injured or killed by the bombing runs of the F-16s.

While all of this was transpiring, Brian staunched Jim's loss of blood with a tourniquet, cleaned and dressed his wound, and stitched it up as best as could be done under the circumstances. While serious in terms of negating Jim's combat ability, Brian could see that his wounds did not pose a significant risk of death or permanent debilitating injury. Having sufficiently stabilized his comrade, Brian quickly turned to his own wound. He deftly cleaned the shrapnel from his forearm, dressed it, and staunched his blood loss with a tourniquet.

Far from dissuading him from further combat, being wounded motivated Brian to take the fight directly to the enemy. As soon as Brian ascertained that Jim could be safely left in his current position, he swapped his 9mm pistol for Jim's M240G heavy machine gun and surveyed the battle scene.

Chad and Eric, the machine gunner and assistant gunner, had managed to join John at the outcrop following Team Bravo's securing of the enemy's forward position. They were now attempting to engage the Al-Qaida fighters in the bunker with machine-gun fire in order to prevent them from concentrating their efforts on blasting Team Bravo with RPGs from their fortified position. Undeterred by that engagement, a tenacious group of Al-Qaida gunmen continued to spider their way through the rocky terrain toward the downed Apache.

As John, Chad, and Eric desperately fired to halt the advancing enemy forces, a pair of F-15s swooped down from the sky with a thundering roar toward the Apache, guns blazing. In a blistering onslaught, their six-barreled, 20mm cannons unleashed a barrage of armor-piercing rounds that sliced through the battle-shocked enemy combatants. The first run killed three Al-Qaida and injured an additional three fighters. The remaining eighteen Al-Qaida fighters then made a fateful decision.

As Brian rushed toward John's position, he could see enemy fighters closing in at full speed on the black, fifty-eight-foot Apache gunship. Shouting a chilling death-cry of "Allah Akbar!" the Al-Qaida militants closed their noose around the Apache. In a brilliant tactical move, they were closing in on the six remaining Rangers before the F-15s could complete additional runs and annihilate them with aerial fire.

John immediately radioed Sean. "Make direct radio contact with the F-16s and tell them we need them here yesterday," John ordered. "We need that bunker taken out ASAP!"

"Yes, sir."

Sean directly contacted the F-16 pilots, bypassing headquarters. "We have an urgent situation on the ground," he advised. "Immediate air bombing support requested. What is estimate to target?"

"Five minutes to target," the senior pilot answered back. "Priority understood."

"That's not good enough!" John roared, mixing in some choice expletives, when Sean relayed him the news.

But he knew that there was nothing further he could do to speed their arrival. They had been called in from a destination in north-central Afghanistan almost 180 miles away and were already flying at Mach 2 speed.

The F-15s attempted a second run but were only able to pick off two Al-Qaida stragglers, one of whom had already been wounded. Due to the urgency of their mission and its call for cannon fire only, the F-15s had not armed themselves with bombs and, as a result, were essentially useless in the battle now unfolding.

After being apprised of the air support situation, Brian told his good friend and platoon leader, John, "I'm willing to risk an approach to the western ridgeline opposite the bunker to divert them."

"That's crazy, Brian. You'll be almost fully exposed to RPG fire from the bunker," John countered.

"Team Bravo can attack the bunker with RPG and machine-gun fire to occupy the Al-Qaida forces there as best they can while I draw fire away from the Apache."

John knew Brian well enough from the attack on Kandahar Airport in Operation Rhino to know that he could not dissuade his friend from this mission. Besides, John was not willing to command Brian to sit idly by while his fellow Rangers suffered grisly deaths.

John made a split-second decision. "Okay, take Chad and Eric with you. I'll radio Sean and have Team Bravo engage the bunker as much as possible from their position. I'd come with you myself, but someone has to be in contact with the F-16s, giving them adjustments to target, if necessary. Good luck, Brian."

Brian did not consider himself a hero. He was just a soldier doing what any other soldier would have done under the circumstances. However, the undeniable fact was that his action, if successful, would save the lives of four beleaguered Rangers, sparing them from a brutal, close-range reckoning with Al-Qaida forces.

Dangerously exposed, Brian, Chad, and Eric brought intense machine-gun fire on the unsuspecting attackers, slaying five and wounding six others in a seven-minute engagement. Each moment of the grisly battle ticked by, second by second, as if lasting an eternity. The pinned Rangers from the downed Apache literally slaughtered the rest of the Al-Qaida fighters in hand-to-hand combat, slashing several to death while suffering two casualties of their own. At the end of the battle, there were only three Al-Qaida fighters taken prisoner. The rest of the so-called jihadists, though wounded, had fought to the death.

During this deadly battle, the two F-16 Fighting Falcons each performed two flybys, narrowly missing the enemy's lair on their first run. After making adjustments directed by John, they succeeded in blasting the bunker into oblivion on their second run. Topping off the successful rescue operation, an evacuation helicopter arrived just in time to save Ben, who by that point was an "urgent surgical" in the words of the Team Bravo medic.

Brian paid a dear, but not unexpected, price for his gallantry. Two minutes before the F-16s arrived, an RPG round exploded meters away from Brian, blanketing him with shrapnel and rendering him unconscious. When he came to, he was at Landstuhl Regional Medical Center in Germany.

"How did Chad and Eric fare?" Brian asked, sipping his Bolivian roast coffee. "I lost contact with them while I was laid up at Landstuhl. Were they wounded by that RPG?"

"They suffered some non-life-threatening lacerations, but you were the one closest to it," John answered. "If I were a civilian, I would say, 'I told you so' and 'The odds were that would happen.' But as a military brother, I can say, 'That was the bravest act of courage that I have ever witnessed!' I'm enormously proud of you. You saved four lives without a doubt."

"John, any of us would have done the same thing in my position."

"No, I didn't write you up for a Silver Star for doing something ordinary. What you did was extraordinary. You earned that Silver Star," John insisted, referring to Brian's receipt of the army's third-highest award for combat valor. "Let's end the debate right there."

Brian soberly nodded, amenable to changing the subject while his mind continued to race through his flashbacks to the scene of battle. Recognizing that the military's decision to award a Silver Star was somewhat subjective, he had humbly accepted it. However, in his mind, Brian truly believed that he had only done what any fellow Ranger of able body would have done to save the lives of comrades in mortal danger. Besides the Silver Star, Brian had received a Purple Heart for sustaining enemy-inflicted wounds in combat.

"How are your folks doing back home in Portsmouth?" Brian asked, pivoting the conversation.

"Real well. My dad's still a Coastie, working in an office rather than out and about on a ship these days. Luckily, he continues to love what he does each day. My mom teaches English at Booker T. Washington High School in Norfolk. Likewise, for her, it's both a mission and a passion."

"I'm glad to hear that," Brian said, still appreciative of the hospitality that they had shown him during Thanksgiving while he and John were seniors at Georgetown.

Besides serving the cadets the best meals that they would eat over the course of their final year of ROTC training together, the company had been gracious, light-hearted, and welcoming. "They're great folks."

"Yeah, guess they did do a decent job keeping me on the straight and narrow," John responded. "My old man sure can swear, though. I think I inherited that from him at birth."

"That's why we chose you as our platoon leader," Brian joked. "You scared the daylight out of all of us with your strings of expletives. Everyone figured, 'If this guy can fight half as well as he can swear, we'll be golden.'"

"Yeah, that's about right. I fight half as well as I swear on the battlefield!"

In actuality, John was one of those natural leaders who connected with his peers and commanded their respect through perpetually exuding strength and optimism and providing constructive support to those around him. He had the rare ability to remain focused on the task at hand amidst physically, emotionally, and mentally trying circumstances—circumstances like those that had confronted his Quick Reaction Force that fateful day last March.

Brian likewise possessed leadership abilities. Unlike John, however, he did not consciously seek to lead and inspire others. Rather, Brian focused on excelling in his role as a combat medic and in providing leadership by example as and when required by the task at hand.

Neither of their contrasting leadership styles had gone unrecognized. Beginning with their freshmen year of ROTC training at Georgetown, their instructor had selected each of them to serve as members of Georgetown's Ranger Challenge Team. The Ranger Challenge was a prestigious annual competition conducted on a regional basis across the United States that pitted the best ROTC teams against each other in completing physical and technical challenges. These ranged from weapons and bridge assembly to M-16 rifle marksmanship and a grenade assault course to a grueling ten-kilometer combat equipment march.

During their senior year, John had led Georgetown's Ranger Challenge Team to a first-place finish out of thirty teams in the mid-Atlantic region competition at Fort A.P. Hill, Virginia, earning a first place Brigade Ranger Challenge Award for Brian and the rest of their team members.

The two became close friends during the course of their officer training, pushing each other to defy their own preconceived limits of what they could accomplish in order to excel as soldiers and as men. Highlighting their grit and determination, Brian and John had finished first and second on their team in the ultra-competitive army ten- miler during their senior year. Equally impressive, they completed the course in less than fifty-four minutes, averaging 5:20 per mile. Together, they had trained intensively for the race, completing speed-workouts on Georgetown's track as well as hill-training on Georgetown's punishing hills during the hot, humid August in Washington following their graduation from National Advanced Leaders Camp (NALC) that July.

Conducted the summer between their junior and senior years, NALC represented the most important training event to that point in their young army careers. The rigorous thirty-five-day camp enhanced their leadership skills and identified their officer potential. It featured squad and platoon situational training exercises; training in nuclear, biological, and chemical weapons; land navigation; individual tactical training; and a field leader's reaction course, which tested their ability to lead squads in navigating through difficult physical obstacles. Both young men had emerged from NALC as proven leaders, confident in their abilities and determined to persevere no matter how daunting the challenges before them.

Brian smiled and said, "You can be a real ham. Remember our Combat Water Survival Training at Ranger School? You came to the pool carrying a rifle and wearing boots, ammo pouches, a pistol belt, and two canteens. Looking you over with a dubious smile, the Ranger instructor asked whether you were all set for the fifteen-meter swim. You nodded your head, even though you knew full well that you could barely doggie-paddle to save your life. So, the RI obligingly blindfolded you before you walked off the three-meter diving board and plunged into the pool as blind as a bat.

"As soon as you hit the water, you started thrashing around like you were going to drown. Just as the medic was about to dive in to drag your sorry butt poolside and administer CPR, you took a deep breath, put your head face down into the water, and kicked like your life depended on it. Let me tell you, bro—that was just about the funniest thing I have ever seen!"

Laden with twenty-five pounds of clothing and equipment, not to mention a rifle in hand, John had painstakingly kicked his way to the opposite end of the pool almost fifty feet away, but John had managed to complete it without taking a breath. That was the kind of courage and determination that had inspired John's battalion commander to choose him as his platoon leader and award him the Distinguished Leadership Award.

"I'm glad you got a kick out of that, Buddy. I'm sure I also entertained the RI more than he was accustomed to. That guy looked like he needed some humor," John reminisced. "In any case, Afghanistan hasn't been testing my CWST skills."

"And Havre de Grace hasn't been testing mine, either, though I did do some water therapy when I first got back. You about ready to head out to rendezvous with Ron, Gabe, and Paul and pick up the tuxes?"

"Sounds like a plan."

With that, they finished their bagels, left a tip, and headed out to destination number two on the day's itinerary: Belvedere Tuxedo Rentals in Baltimore.

CHAPTER 4

A twenty-three-year-old woman with flowing brown hair and eyes to match awakened to the soft rays of sunlight flickering through her shades. Cracking them open and peering onto the sparkling waters of the Potomac from her apartment in Old Town Alexandria, she felt energized to begin what she felt would be one of the most memorable and meaningful experiences of her life.

She ignored the detailed itinerary of her wedding day lying on her nightstand and instead gazed at the picture of a beaming girl standing beside a Maasai warrior. The warrior bore fierce face paint but sported laughing eyes that instantly erased any pretense of danger. The girl was brilliantly arrayed, displaying a multi-colored beaded bracelet on her forearm and a luxuriously woven beaded necklace around her neck.

Kimeli did make it back in time from his hunt, Beth remembered, recalling how Kimeli, still arrayed in his warrior clothing, had rushed to the village to see Brian and her on her last evening in Kenya.

She and Brian eagerly greeted Kimeli outside their missionary boma, *a thatched hut surrounded by a circle of thorny bushes for protection from hyenas and other nocturnal predators.*

After embracing his friends, Kimeli had insisted that Beth put on her wedding regalia and pose for a picture beside his dark and handsome figure. Lithe in build, Kimeli's bright red shuka flowed with warrior splendor, matched by black-striped red cloth draped around his shoulder and a colorful belt with green, yellow, orange, and red bands mirroring the beaded colors of his hunting necklace.

"We are Maasai family—brother and sister," Kimeli pronounced, smiling so broadly that Beth could see the gap in his lower mouth from his missing incisors.

"I hope to come to the great celebration of your wedding with my good friend, Brian," Kimeli said. "I can see God's love and goodness in your hearts."

She and Brian both instantly blushed.

"Please take our picture before your blood drains from your cheeks," Kimeli implored. "Then, Beth will take our picture—one warrior hunter and one missionary warrior for Christ—with your blushing face beside me as red as my shuka!"

★ ★ ★

Beth's eyes sparkled with the same laughter and light as Kimeli's rich brown eyes had that evening eleven years ago as she slowly reached inside a worn leather bag adorned with small glass beads.

My dreams from that day are finally coming true, she thought excitedly, as with full eyes she drew a stunning beaded necklace from the bag and placed it around her neck.

As she did so, all the concerns with her detailed itinerary for the day faded away, and her mind was transported back in time to the most beautiful dawn she had ever witnessed, embracing Brian atop a majestic hill overlooking the savannah.

CHAPTER 5

As John turned onto I-95 South heading toward Baltimore, he glanced over at the man sitting next to him. What he saw filled him with both pride and sadness.

He saw a man whose head was unbowed, who had not wavered in the face of adversity, and who had chosen to risk his life in order to save the lives of fellow soldiers. He also saw a man who had paid a heavy price for this decision.

The scars on Brian's neck and the side of his jaw were evidence of the shrapnel that had torn into his body. The medical dangers posed by the shrapnel—toxic metals, infection, inflammation, and muscle and nerve damage—had required its removal by head and neck surgeons at Landstuhl, the most advanced medical treatment center for coalition war casualties outside of the United States.

John beheld a dear friend who had never questioned or regretted his battlefield decision to risk his life for his Ranger brothers. Rather, Brian had written to his buddies in the field, regretting that he would not have the "privilege" of returning to the theater of combat to fight alongside them due to unforeseen medical circumstances:

I have been advised by the good doctors here at Landstuhl to schedule immediate surgery in the U.S. at Walter Reed for purposes of removing a large malignant mole on my neck. The malignancy was detected in an examination and follow-up biopsy during the course of my treatment here. The surgery—which they call Mohs Micrographic Surgery—will remove the cancerous layers of skin using microscopic mapping and a scalpel. I don't want you guys worrying at all about this. The doctors believe it to be an isolated malignant mole (called melanoma) and tell me that the surgery is highly effective.

Following surgery, they expect that I will be free of cancer but, nevertheless, have advised follow-up evaluation in the U.S. In any event, my only regret is that I cannot, at this time, return to you and my other brothers to complete our mission. I pray that God will watch over and bless all of you.

In looking at Brian, John also felt a pang of remorse that he had not been able to visit his best friend during the course of his treatment and post-surgical observation at Landstuhl and then at Walter Reed Army Medical Center. For shortly after the completion of Operation Anaconda, John had found himself swept up by a powerful current of events in Afghanistan that demanded his undivided attention.

John had been selected to help train and reconstitute the core of the Afghan National Army under the ultimate command of Hamid Karzai, chairman of the Afghan Interim Authority. Three months later, John was elated when a national grand council elected Hamid Karzai—the Pashtun leader who had fought alongside U.S. Special Forces to free his country from Taliban rule—as president of Afghanistan. Along with Green Berets and other elite U.S. troops, John had helped to form a small but crucial cadre of well-trained Afghan officers from a disparate group of recruits who represented diverse ethnic groups, spoke different languages, and, in some cases, bore long-standing enmities toward other ethnicities represented by their fellow officers-in-training.

During his only authorized military leave coinciding with Brian's convalescence, John had married his high school sweetheart, Ashley, in Afghanistan. The wedding was conducted in a simple ceremony by a military chaplain at Bagram Air Base. Although it had been a tough decision knowing that their families, their non-military friends, and John's best man would be unable to attend, the strains of a prolonged overseas deployment and the uncertainties of the dangers lying ahead had led the couple to push forward with the military nuptial. As a symbol of his closest friend's absence from the wedding, John had arranged for a single sheathed sword to lie on the ground as he and Ashley passed underneath the traditional sword arch of drawn military swords and exited the chapel.

Sitting beside his best friend, John recalled his thoughts as Brian lay immobile atop that desolate mountain ridge in the Shah-i-Kot Valley of Paktika Province. As he had watched Brian's evacuation by helicopter, he thought that he might never see Brian alive again. Seeing him now—in person—was powerful, causing John to appreciate just how much Brian meant to his life.

"I want to apologize to you, Brian, for not being there with you during your surgeries. I wasn't there in person, but I sure was there in spirit," John said, swallowing from the unexpected emotion he had in uttering those long-stored words of apology.

Brian gave John a reassuring pat on his shoulder and smiled. "I knew that you wanted to be there, John. You had more important things to do than visit a guy lying on his back and eating soft food in some military hospital. You had obligations to your country, to the people you served with, and most importantly—lest either of us forget—to the number one woman in your life. Beth and I would have done the same thing under those circumstances. I'm really glad that you didn't decide to visit and reschedule your wedding."

John shook his head sheepishly, not quite believing that Brian would have done the same thing had their situations been reversed.

"Besides, it wasn't like I didn't have plenty of people to talk to each day. I actually got to meet some real war heroes."

John nodded and looked over at Brian. "Didn't you meet Gabe at Landstuhl?"

"Yes, sure did. Gabe is quite a guy . . . "

Delta Sergeant Gabe Sheffield, alongside a small team of fellow U.S. and British Special Forces and a separate team of Northern Alliance fighters, had continuously risked his life trying to recover the body of the slain CIA operative, John Michael Spann, in the infamous uprising at Qala-i-Jangi following the fall of Mazar-e-Sharif. After Al-Qaida terrorists, including John Walker Lindh, overpowered CIA operatives Mike Spann and Dave Tyson and their Northern Alliance prison guards to take control of the Qala-i-Jangi fortress, a United States lieutenant colonel quickly dispatched a team of elite Special Forces to rescue the two CIA operatives, whose status and location within the fortress remained unknown.

Dodging intense Al-Qaida small-arms fire, as well as shrapnel fragmented from ordnance dropped by friendly air support, Gabe and his team engaged in close quarter, room-to-room combat in the southern half of the fortress. Despite moving into enemy-occupied parts of the fortress without knowledge of its layout, the team furiously battled the fanatical Al-Qaida fighters. They realized each second was precious and let the tenacious enemy feel every ounce of their ferocity.

Fortunately, Dave Tyson had managed to escape from the fortress soon after Gabe's team had been deployed. Unfortunately, despite their herculean efforts, by the time that the Northern Alliance team found Mike Spann, it was too late. They found his lifeless, brutally tortured body bearing multiple bullets to his spine and the back of his neck.

Enraged, Gabe and his team had avenged themselves in a withering attack on Spann's brutal killers who, facing inevitable defeat, nevertheless preferred death to surrender. Despite gunshot wounds to his left arm and lower leg, Gabe continued to fight into the darkness of the night until a misplaced Hellfire missile slammed into adjoining fortress walls and rendered him unconscious.

"Yes, Gabe is one solid guy," Brian added. "This may sound strange, but he helped inspire me to recover quickly and get back on my feet as soon as I could."

"I wouldn't question that for a second," John responded. "He's a rare breed—someone we all can admire. How is he holding up?"

"He's doing really well, all things considered. He lost some hearing when his eardrums were ruptured by the missile's impact, and he has limited range of motion in his left arm. Overall, though, he's in good health and spirits and is happy to be back in the States working as a purchaser for Lockheed."

"That's really good to hear. I'm looking forward to meeting this almost legendary guy in person. How about Ron and Paul—what are they up to these days?"

"Ron's finishing up his second year of med school at B.U.; he's thinking about going into orthopedic surgery. Paul is a legislative staffer on the Hill, hoping to run for Congress himself one day."

"Good for them. Given everything that's happened since graduation, I haven't even had a chance to keep up with those guys." At this, John became silent, lost in thought.

Less than ten minutes later, the Georgetown graduates and their newfound friend, Gabe, met in a spirited reunion at Belvedere Tuxedo Rentals. Ron and Paul got to see John, a man with whom they had spent many senior year nights at the Tombs and other local G-Town hangouts. As for Gabe, his contagious enthusiasm and remarkable story—which Brian had previously shared with each of his groomsmen—made him an instant celebrity.

After securing their wedding day accoutrements, the four men made their way to the parking lot. Their final, pre-wedding destination of the day would be Edgar's Billiards Club at Baltimore's Inner Harbor: the perfect place to play a couple games of pool and grab a casual lunch.

CHAPTER 6

Sensitive to the sound of the unfamiliar car approaching her home, a middle-aged woman of slight build and careful demeanor lifted the curtain to her living room window and peered outside. A black Chrysler came to a stop by the edge of the driveway to her modest three-bedroom, brick home in Columbia, Maryland. A young man dressed in a U.S. Army Ranger uniform stepped out of the car, removed his tan beret, and approached the stone walkway leading up to her door.

The woman let out a slight gasp and clutched the handle of her front door. As the doorbell rang, she tried to compose herself and slowly opened the door. With a glaze over her eyes, she looked up at the young man before her but, instead, in a terrifying flashback, saw the faces of three uniformed men who had visited her home thirteen months before.

★ ★ ★

"Ma'am, are you Mrs. Johnson? I am Captain Frank Tettleton of the Seventy-Fifth Ranger regiment, Third Battalion, stationed at Fort Benning. With me are First Lieutenant Isaac Kessler, Army Chaplain Corps, and First Lieutenant Bruce Holzig, Army Medical Corps—each also from the Seventy-Fifth Ranger regiment, Third Battalion, Fort Benning. I regret to inform you that your son, First Lieutenant Brian Johnson, has been seriously injured *in combat with enemy forces in Afghanistan and has been air evacuated from a theater-deployed hospital to Landstuhl Regional Medical Center in Germany for immediate surgery. Lieutenant Johnson sustained shrapnel wounds to his face and neck. Further surgical evaluation at Landstuhl Regional Medical Center is required at this time in order to determine whether or not his injuries are life-threatening . . . "*

Overwhelmed with the memory, the woman stumbled to the ground in shock before hearing a voice call out, "Mrs. Johnson? Mrs. Johnson? Are you okay?"

It was the young man who had just driven up to her home. "Mrs. Johnson, I'm Randy Clark, a Ranger friend of your son, Brian. I'm sorry if I alarmed you being in uniform and all. I just arrived from Camp Cooke in Taji, Iraq, ma'am, where I was stationed following my deployment in Afghanistan. I flew directly into Atlanta and then connected to Dulles. I'm used to traveling in uniform, and I didn't have a chance to change into civilian dress. I'm really sorry once again, Mrs. Johnson."

Brian's mother paused for a moment before putting on a tense smile. "No worries, Randy. That's quite okay. I don't know what came over me. I'm Laura Johnson. Please, come in and make yourself at home. Brian let us know you'd be coming, and we're delighted that you came all this way for the wedding. My husband is finishing up a prayer meeting at the church. He should be back home shortly."

Mrs. Johnson motioned for Randy to take a seat on the living room sofa and offered to get him a drink.

"No, thank you. I'm fine, Mrs. Johnson. I don't know exactly how to say this, but I've had quite a bit of time to think it over on my way here . . . Mrs. Johnson, I would not be here today were it not for Brian's actions. If you would permit me, ma'am, I'd like to tell you how your son saved my life in Operation Anaconda."

Brian's mother hesitated for a moment, then took a seat beside Randy. She braced herself, knowing in her heart that, as his mother, she needed to know exactly what her son had done that day and what he had endured.

Nodding, she answered, "Yes, thank you so much, Randy. That would mean a lot to me, and it would perhaps give me some peace—or, at least, some closure—knowing exactly what happened that day. You see, Brian never talks about the war. Stephen and I went to Brian's award ceremony down at Fort Benning, where he received the Silver Star. The officer gentleman awarding him the Silver Star said something about 'conspicuous gallantry in risking his life to save the lives of fellow soldiers under attack.' But more than that, I really do not know."

As she said this, Mrs. Johnson suddenly felt somewhat embarrassed—and even ashamed—that she did not already know what Randy was about to tell her.

"Mrs. Johnson, I was one of those fellow soldiers. Ma'am, from what Brian has told me, you are a woman of faith. The motto of the U.S. Army Ranger Association—taken from Isaiah chapter six, verse eight—says a lot about the character of your son and what he did in volunteering to go to war to serve this country in a time of need. It also speaks volumes about what he did in volunteering that day to risk his life in order to save my life and the lives of three other Rangers. If I may, it says, 'And I heard the voice of the Lord saying, 'Whom shall I send, and who will go for us?' Then I said, 'Here I am! Send me.'"

Randy proceeded to tell the entire story of how Brian had saved his life and the lives of at least three other soldiers that day, beginning with the RPG fire that brought down his Apache AH-64 helicopter and ending with the four Rangers left standing when the battle ended.

When Randy finished recounting the battle, Mrs. Johnson nodded her head and thanked him, her mind still quietly processing everything he had said.

"You know," she said after a few moments of silence, "Brian has always loved to help people, especially underdogs—yes, ever since he was a boy. He was an amazing child."

Looking at Randy, she could see that he was absorbed with what she was saying. She decided to share with him a story from Brian's childhood that was on her mind.

"When Brian was just eight years old, he watched a news story about a little girl who had been injured in a car accident. The poor girl's kidneys were failing her, and she was hooked up to a dialysis machine. Brian came into the kitchen, where I was cooking dinner, and asked whether we could go to the hospital. Somewhat alarmed, I looked my boy over but didn't see anything wrong with him. He had no scrapes, bruises, or other telltale signs. Rather, he was brimming with vitality and life. And so, I asked him what had happened.

"With the sheepish half-smile of a boy who had unwittingly frightened his poor mother, Brian explained that he wanted to go to the hospital to have one of his kidneys removed. He wanted the doctors to give one to the little girl on TV who needed a kidney transplant. My, he was such a sweet boy."

"That's a really special memory, Mrs. Johnson. Maybe that's what got Brian interested in medicine," Randy offered with a smile.

"Yes, perhaps," Mrs. Johnson mused, reminiscing. "Brian seemed to be interested in helping sick and injured people, especially children, from the time he was a boy."

Randy nodded, listening intently.

"One day, when Brian was in third grade, I received a call from a lunchroom attendant at his school. She asked if there were any financial problems at our home. Taken aback, I answered no and asked her why she had raised the question. She told me that Brian had been borrowing money all week from her for lunch.

"When Brian returned home from school later that day, I asked him whether he was losing his lunch money or spending it on soda or candy or whether a bully was taking it away from him each day. He told me, 'No, Mom, I'm giving it to help kids who are fighting for their lives.' As it turns out, Brian was donating all of his lunch money each day to a school drive to raise money for children with leukemia. He explained that those kids needed it more than he did. Yes, that's the kind of boy we raised."

"Thank you for raising a son with that kind of character, Mrs. Johnson," Randy said, looking into her eyes with deep gratitude. "In some ways, I owe my life to you and your husband as much as I do to Brian. As they say, 'The apple doesn't fall far from the tree.'"

"Thank you, Randy. You don't know how much your words mean to me," Mrs. Johnson said, brushing back tears.

Randy offered her a comforting pat on the shoulder and then hugged her. Little could he know the deeper reason for how emotional the subject of her son was to her these days.

CHAPTER 7

At La Madeleine in Old Town Alexandria, Beth's older sister and also the matron of honor, Lisa, stood up and addressed her fellow bridesmaids.

"It's great to see all of you here today for this breakfast in honor of my lovely baby sister, Beth. As we all know, she is marrying a tremendous guy—some would say 'the man of her dreams'—later today. In putting this together, I wanted to add a dash of suspense, humor, and yes, *embarrassment* to the occasion. So, I'm going to ask each of you to share a story about Beth this morning which you have never dared to tell us. The story must be funny or embarrassing to Beth—and preferably both, which fits the bill perfectly for this first story I'll share."

Lisa scanned the faces of her fellow bridesmaids. Judging from the looks on their faces, they had more than a couple of stories from which to choose. Mischievously glancing over at her sister, she observed that Beth had a slightly bemused look on her face evidencing uncertainty as to the type and degree of embarrassment these stories held in store.

"Fortunately for Beth, there are only four of us," Lisa added with a playful smile. "Beth and I go back quite a way—to her birth, actually—so there are a lot of good stories from which to choose. But it didn't take me long to settle on the one I'm about to share with you. This entails, shall we say, a *unique* cultural experience my sister and I had some years ago.

"It was only our second day at the Maasai village during our medical mission trip to Kenya, and we certainly wanted to make a good impression.

"Before us stood fourteen strikingly proud, sinewy Maasai warriors, called *morani*. They were clothed in bright red tunics and adorned with colorful anklets, bracelets, and multi-ringed, beaded necklaces. Not only they, but the entire village, stood before Beth, another missionary family, and me. To round out the attention, several esteemed elders, clad in colorful red and purple tunics and shawls and wearing ornate beaded necklaces and earrings, watched us approvingly.

"That day, even their fine fashion was outshone by that of the young warriors. With red, clay-colored hair, arms, and legs striped orange with red ochre, and tunics sporting gold and silver ornaments, the *morani* were looking fine. Their entire tribe admired the radiant warriors—especially the beautiful, young, Maasai women, who, as we later learned, hoped one day to be chosen by these *morani* as the first of their many wives.

"For just a few moments, there was complete silence. Then we heard low, guttural grunts come from the chests and throats of several *morani*, filling the air with a rhythm we had never heard before. These grunts soon gave way to improvisation and overlapping voices. We were nearly hypnotized by the blended rhythm of men grunting in a deep, rich base while the *morani* leader told a story of a great lion hunt. All of us newcomers were entranced, not even realizing that the main spectacle was still to come.

"A *moran* suddenly leaped more than three feet into the air. He then followed it with a second leap that was just as spectacular. As soon as he returned to his place in the row of warriors, another *moran* dazzled us all with a series of deft bounds. Then, just like the previous warrior, he quickly receded from attention, returning to stand side by side among the warriors. Meanwhile, the non-leaping *morani* swayed back and forth and sang, providing a musical backdrop for these acrobatic feats. This continued until all fourteen warriors had wowed us with their strength and agility.

"The lead *morani* singer, a friendly young teenager named Kimeli, then invited us as their special guests from America to share American singing and dancing with the Maasai people. Mortified at the thought, my sister tried to shrink back out of view. I, on the other hand, couldn't take my eyes off of Kimeli's contagious smile, which led me to volunteer Beth's talents.

"'Beth is a Belvedette!' I cried out to sixty uncomprehending Maasai. 'I mean, Beth dances for her school back at home, and she is a wonderful cheerleader. She jumps and cheers!'

"After a year of trying, I, the bolder, older sister, had finally persuaded Beth to try out for the school dance troupe and cheerleading squad. She was a novice, having just made the cheerleading team that spring and barely knew a few basic routines.

"Their expectations as high as their leaps, the *morani* were excited that a fellow jumper was purportedly among them. 'Please sing and jump for us!' a Maasai chief implored in British-sounding English, gesturing for my sister to join them on stage.

"Beth at first demurred, looking quite overwhelmed, but then I saw her lock eyes with Brian. She changed her mind in an instant.

"'Okay, let's give it a try,' Beth said with a voice that didn't fully hide her nerves. Nonetheless, she rose to her feet and joined the *morani* at center stage.

"Gazing out at the expectant faces of Kimeli and the rest of the Maasai people, she completely blanked. She stood there for an awkwardly long time in silence, looking to be deep in thought, before finally saying, 'Okay . . . okay . . . I have it.' Apparently, 'it' referred to a single dance troupe routine choreographed to C+C Music Factory's 'Everybody Dance Now.'

"With everyone deep in a respectful silence, Beth blurted out in a loud, slightly off-key voice, the embarrassingly emphatic and repetitive lyrics, throwing in energetic but vertically challenged leaps during each refrain. Upon landing her final jump, the Maasai had stupefied looks on their faces, and we were all just standing in place in shocked silence.

"At first, the Maasai had no idea how to react. Their stunned silence, however, soon gave way to a chorus of giggling and amused chatter. Then, they started to point in an animated fashion toward my twelve-year old sister. Beth looked completely rattled. Representing her country, her church, her family, her would-be-boyfriend, and who knows what else, she had done the equivalent of a belly flop at the Olympics.

"With the eyes of Kimeli and the entire Maasai village upon her, Beth made a beeline in the opposite direction. Her hands to her scarlet face, she barely avoided colliding with a startled goat before darting headfirst into the *boma* where we were staying, supposedly as honorary guests. With her stage exit complete, the Maasai people, joined by a missionary or two—including possibly me—erupted in full-throated laughter."

"Yes, that made your day," Beth said, laughing good-naturedly at the naivete of her actions. "That's definitely on my top ten list of embarrassing moments."

"The rest of us have not had the benefit of forethought," Christy, Beth's best friend from childhood, said. "However, I think it's safe to say that we can add to the list. Beth and I starred as Nancy Sykes and Miss Betsy, respectively, in the fourth-grade play, *Oliver Twist*. As part of the play, we had to sing and dance to the song, 'I'd Do Anything,' along with Oliver and The Artful Dodger. Beth had quite a crush on Andrew, who played the dashing, larger-than-life character of The Artful Dodger. Apparently, as we all soon found out, her love did not go unrequited.

"One day after rehearsal, a stagehand found Andrew backstage on one knee holding Beth's hand and singing, 'I'd Do Anything' to her. By the end of the next day, the story had broken out to just about everybody in the fourth grade. It was one of the big romance stories of our fourth-grade year, as you might imagine."

"That's cute, that's really cute. We'll give you credit for it, even though I independently heard about it from one of my sixth-grade sources at the time," Lisa said lightheartedly. "All right, who's the next volunteer? A special prize will be awarded to anyone who tops the Maasai tale on the scale of embarrassment."

"Okay, let's try this one," Stephanie offered. "While we were in college together, Miss RN helped organize a big blood drive by the American Red Cross to stock up in case of natural disasters or terrorist attacks. Beth persuaded school officials at Washington-Lee High School in Arlington to become a sponsor of the blood drive. She also convinced my cousin, Tony, an eleventh grader at the school, to be the student leader of the blood drive and encourage students to sign up and participate with parental consent.

"Tony had never participated in a blood drive before and could not remember the last time he had ever gotten a shot. However, being a big, tough guy and leader of the blood drive, Tony had little choice but to participate himself. To give you a sense of Tony and his macho self-image, he wrestled, hunted gators down in Florida with my uncle during summer vacations, and idolized Arnold Schwarzenegger, quipping *Terminator* quotes on a daily basis. So, little did Tony—or anyone else—suspect what was about to transpire.

"Having cajoled two-thirds of his classmates into participating in the drive by various means, Tony proudly strolled over to the blood station to donate his blood. After dutifully collecting his parental consent, Beth asked Tony the standard question, 'Have you ever experienced any problems or had any qualms with having your blood drawn?' Tony dismissed it out of hand with an exaggerated and exasperated shake of his head and impatiently held out his arm. With that settled, Beth matter-of-factly sterilized the needlepoint on Tony's forearm, asked him to clench his fist, and proceeded to draw his blood.

"While Beth was drawing Tony's blood, she observed his face lose some of its color. When questioned about it, 'Big Ego' Tony insisted he was perfectly fine and demanded that she finish drawing his blood.

"Beth obliged. As soon as she removed the needle, applied pressure to the needle point, and bandaged it, Tony began his typical muscle-man stride toward the school's weight room. However, before he had taken three steps, he staggered sidewise, his face pale with fright. As Beth rose to her feet, Tony waved her off, saying between panicked breaths, 'I'm fine; I'm fine. Just a little woozy . . .'

"With that, he made a hasty beeline for a water fountain just inside the gymnasium. Seconds later, Beth heard someone shout, 'Tony's dead! Tony's dead!'

"A terrified classmate had apparently found Tony lying on his back, with eyes closed, a few feet inside of the gym and pronounced him dead to everyone within earshot. Beth gasped in horror and rushed inside the gym, defibrillator in one hand and her full medical bag in the other. She braced herself, preparing for the worst—cardiac arrest.

"Meanwhile, some kids clasped their heads in horror, while others, thinking Tony had simply passed out from fright, seized their chance for revenge. They took turns announcing, 'The *Terminator* has terminated!' and 'The wicked witch is dead!' to a mixture of gasps and amusement.

"Of course, Tony had simply fainted from having his blood drawn, and Beth soon revived the 'tough guy' with smelling salts. He sat up, perfectly okay—except for his immensely bruised ego.

"For the remainder of his high school days, Tony was the laughingstock of the school, and our big-hearted Florence Nightingale blamed herself for the entire incident. From my perspective, it was a riot."

"All right, good job, Stephanie," Lisa complimented. "You just stole the inside track with one lap to go."

"Yeah, thanks, Stephanie. I certainly needed to be reminded of that," Beth said in good humor. "At least, there is only one more story for me to brave."

"We saved the best for last, right, Kathryn?" Lisa asked.

"But, of course," Kathryn agreed. "The December before last, Beth enlisted my help to produce a video to send to Brian while he was stationed in Afghanistan. Of course, the theme of the video was 'Christmas in Arlington.' Consistent with that theme, Beth sewed a red and white Jessica outfit from scratch for herself.

"For anyone who is not a Santa Claus trivia buff, Jessica is the name of the woman who married Kris Kringle and became Mrs. Claus. Then, Beth somehow convinced me to dress up as a green elf and to arrange for my husband, Burt, to dress up as Santa Claus and come to her house to videotape a holiday scene for Brian. To top it off, she made an adorable Santa Claus hat for her Maine Coon cat, Snowflake.

"So, there we were, all gathered together in the living room of Beth's townhouse, along with her next-door neighbor, Gina, who was manning the video camera. Beth, dressed as Jessica, was standing in the foreground introducing everyone: Burt Jenkins, sitting next to the Christmas tree starring as Santa Claus; me, holding up two gift-wrapped Christmas presents for Brian while starring as Santa's elf of the year; and, last but not least, Snowflake, wearing an adorable Santa Claus hat while cradled in Beth's arms.

"As Beth proceeded to deliver a sweet message to Brian wishing him and the troops a safe and Merry Christmas, she gently deposited Snowflake into Burt's lap. Unfortunately, Beth did not foresee that her sociable feline, who was fast friends with Burt, would be unable to recognize him in his Santa Claus outfit.

"Terrified of the bearded stranger, scaredy-cat glared her yellow eyes, hissed, and viciously extended her claws. Burt helplessly yelped out in pain and proceeded to release Snowflake from his grasp. Fascinated by the flashing lights of the Christmas tree and wanting to disappear from sight, Snowflake sprang headfirst into the tree, knocking it clear off its stand. All of the Christmas lights short-circuited and, to top things off, they threw off bright white sparks in the process, briefly causing an electrical fire. That is, until Beth and I smothered it with a nearby rug, which was promptly singed, producing a rich, smoky smell to spice up the season. This, mind you, was all immortalized on tape for generations to come.

"After we managed to put out the fire and recover our senses, we decided that Brian would actually get a kick out of the tape, so we sent it to him in Afghanistan. Months later, we learned that Brian had shared the tape with his entire platoon, who kidded him that, under the circumstances, he would be safer with them in Afghanistan than he would be back at home—"

"If only that had proven true," Beth inadvertently blurted out.

For a few moments, her mind wandered back to the long, anxious nights she had endured beginning the very day that Brian first deployed to Afghanistan.

Each night before falling asleep, Beth opened the drawer to her nightstand and re-read the letter that Brian had handed her the morning he left to fly back to Afghanistan. The letter recounted how much Brian loved Beth and would miss her while stationed in Afghanistan. Remarkably mature for a letter written by a twenty-two-year-old, it stated that—God willing and assuming Beth's love endured his twelve-month deployment—Brian would return to Arlington, Virginia, to build a life with her. Brian stressed to her that he did not, for a moment, question whether his service to his country was worth the sacrifice, the danger, or the hardship of separation from loved ones such as herself.

"Serving my country in this manner completes and affirms who I am as a man," he had written. "I could not—in good conscience—shirk my duty to my country and its safety, even to be with you at this time. There are times in

everyone's life when he or she is tested, and that is when our character is forged or, having previously been forged, is refined and honed into a wonderfully resplendent example to others. I am truly excited at the opportunity to share my fervor for my God, my country, and its ideals with my Ranger brothers in a land filled with men, women, and children who are yearning for a freer, safer, and more humane way of life: free from terror, debilitating mines, and religious and sexist oppression."

Brian's letter had correctly predicted that their separation would be hardest upon Beth and his family. Despite her resolution to be strong, every time Beth answered her phone during Brian's deployment, she bit her lip and whispered, "Please, God, let everything be okay."

And then it came—the heart-rending call she had dreaded. She had fielded the phone with trembling hands, with Brian's sobbing mother on the other end. This all transpired on the unforgettable afternoon of March 27, 2002, soon after three uniformed officers had solemnly walked up Mrs. Johnson's front steps and informed her of Brian's life-threatening, battlefield injuries and hospitalization.

However, unlike many of the brave men and women who served in Afghanistan or Iraq, the same bright, loving man I clutched in my arms at the airport returned to me, Beth thought, reminding herself of the greater weight many loved ones of deceased soldiers had to bear. She was resolved to continue in thankfulness for each day she was blessed to spend with Brian. With that mindset, she consciously refused to allow herself to dwell on the negatives but, instead, trusted that God's will would unfold in their intertwined lives.

"Brian returned home, and for that, I'm very grateful. And I'm truly grateful to all of you for sharing those special memories with me," Beth pronounced in a firm tone of voice.

On that bittersweet note, Lisa gave her sister a comforting hug. "When Brian came home, no one could have taken better care of him. Your love truly healed him," Lisa whispered to Beth as they embraced.

"Thank you, Sis. His love helped to heal me, too," Beth whispered back.

Lisa paused, doing her best to compose herself before addressing Beth in the company of her closest friends, "Beth, I couldn't be prouder of you as a sister. Your amazingly warm spirit and compassion for others have inspired me. I saw the joy in your eyes when you celebrated the recovery of Maasai children and the pain in them when a Maasai child suffering from tuberculosis didn't pull through.

"Most memorable is how you came to a decision to dedicate your career to serving the underserved in medicine. Our family was on its first medical mission trip abroad, in Soweto, South Africa, traveling along a highway from Johannesburg to Soweto. A young, black girl on her bicycle swerved into the highway and was struck by a speeding Mercedes, which slowed and then fled the scene. My father immediately pulled over to assist the girl, and another man in a dilapidated car pulled up beside us.

"The girl was barely conscious and was in really bad shape. She appeared to have broken her hip, injured her spine, and broken both her legs. The man in the car beside us, named Nthato, called an ambulance. However, he told us it could take over forty minutes for the 'black' ambulance to arrive. To our astonishment, he explained that if the girl had been white, a whites-only ambulance would have arrived within minutes.

"Focusing on the increasingly serious task at hand, my father put his orthopedic surgeon hat on and assessed her condition. Once done, he turned to us with deep concern etched across his face.

"'She can't be moved without a stretcher,' he warned. 'We have no choice but to wait for the ambulance.'

"While we stood there desperately hoping and praying for the ambulance to arrive, this poor girl—whose name we later saw in the papers was Isoke—suddenly stopped breathing and passed away.

"That night, Beth, you told us that you wanted to dedicate your life to helping people like Isoke, those who otherwise would never receive the medical treatment they deserved as children of God. You wanted to make a difference. And you have in so many ways—in your work as an RN, in medical mission trips, and in helping organize and participate in charitable events. I am really blessed to have a sister like you!"

Visibly moved, Beth hugged her sister again, wiping away tears. "You're the best sister I could ever have. And I'm blessed to have all of you here, too, as my soulmate friends."

"You're awesome! We love you, Beth," Christy cried out, whose sentiment was echoed in a flurry of sincerely felt emotion, coupled with warm embraces of their dear friend.

Once Beth had returned the hugs and managed to compose herself, she said, "Love you guys and your roasts, but only one of you can be crowned the winner. So, drumroll please . . . "

"Sister drummer starting drumroll," Lisa said lightheartedly, mimicking the sound. "Gentle ladies, the winner of the "Roast Beth to Embarrassment Competition" is . . . Stephanie! And the coveted prize that comes with it: one timeless copy of the Snowball video!"

A round of applause ensued, followed by a delicious breakfast of made-to-order omelets.

CHAPTER 8

B rian's father warmly greeted Deacon Peralta, the longest-serving deacon at Columbia's First Baptist Church, and welcomed her to the church's weekly prayer meeting. "Jean, thank you so much for leading the Newcomer's retreat to Camp Fraser last weekend. I have received so many calls and emails this past week from new believers thanking the church—and you, in particular—for having brought them together in such a rich and nurturing environment for Bible study, prayer, outdoor activities, and fellowship."

"Thank you, Pastor Steve. It was a privilege to organize the retreat, and I very much enjoyed the entire experience," Jean answered. "It was so rewarding to see members of our congregation enjoy each other's company and genuinely bond and fellowship together. I have some great pictures of the event, which I'd like to share with our congregation on Sunday, if that works with you."

"That would be wonderful," Stephen replied.

In his sincere and personable manner, the thin, gray-haired pastor welcomed each of the other four deacons to the meeting and opened with a general prayer of praise and thanksgiving. He concluded his prayer by asking for God's guidance in ministering to the needs of their congregation.

"Lord, You have said, *'For where two or three are gathered in my name, there am I among them.'*[2] Please be with us in a special way today; give us discernment, sensitivity, and love in addressing the needs of Your flock. We ask that, in these petitions we offer up before You today, Your perfect will be done."

He then invited each of the deacons to bring the prayer requests and praises of members of their congregation. Through letters, emails, calls, and visits to homes, hospitals, and hospices during the course of the week, the deacons had learned the needs of their church brethren. In addition, they had received welcome news of answered prayers and thanksgiving. They presently brought all of these before the pastor and their fellow deacons for discussion and prayer.

Stephen felt a special gratitude toward his congregation for the many letters, calls, and emails he had received that week congratulating him and his wife on Brian's upcoming wedding, which now was just hours away. He would personally respond to each person, just as he had to every person who had communicated thoughts to him over the past thirty-two years.

To those grieving for loved ones, Pastor Steve sent letters of condolences before visiting them. To those who were depressed, lonely, or laden with worry, he sent letters of encouragement, inviting them to join church members for fellowship and support. And to those who shared thanks or praise, he sent joyful letters and rejoiced before the congregation in their good news.

The pastor was a man who endeared himself to nearly everyone he met through his simple goodness and his desire to help others. His character and compassion had helped mold those around him to be

---

"men for others"—serving neighbors and strangers alike, in the true tradition of Christ.

Toward the end of their meeting, Deacon Peralta rose and brought the prayer box over to Stephen. The prayer box contained anonymous prayer requests from members of their congregation. Stephen opened the first one and shared it with the deacons:

> *Please pray for healing in my marriage. My wife and I are newlyweds who were married last September, but already the communication between us is breaking down. My wife accuses me of being married to my job. I feel she is not grateful for the long hours I put in to pay the bills. She also does not understand my need to spend time with the boys on the weekends. She says she doesn't feel the same emotional intimacy with me that we had before we were married. I know we love each other, but it's hard to make each other feel that way. I'd prefer not to identify myself, but here is an email address that you can use if you'd like . . . I'd like to get your advice, Pastor Steve, as a man of God yourself, regarding what I should do.*

"The first year of marriage," Stephen began, "is a crucial time for a husband and wife to build their relationship. As you know, in Deuteronomy 24:5, God instructed the ancient Israelites in this regard, stating, 'When a man is newly married, he shall not go out with the army or be liable for any other public duty. He shall be free at home one year to be happy with his wife whom he has taken.'"

"Yes, this man needs to make his wife his primary focus," Deacon Fullam opined in a stern voice.

"Agreed, but we must gently instruct him in God's love, rather than condemn him," Stephen explained. "During my first year of marriage, I similarly had to learn this lesson from others. I was an assistant pastor at Cherrydale Baptist Church, fresh out of seminary school, and eager to travel the world to evangelize it for Christ.

"One month after I married Laura, I began to plan a three-week mission trip to the slums of Calcutta. I intended that Laura and I would stay with a missionary who had been based in India for several years. There, we would minister, along with the other mission team members from Cherrydale and local churches, to people on the street.

"It was all perfectly planned in my mind—that is, until I consulted with Laura, and she categorically rejected the entire idea. Laura wanted us to focus on finding a home near Cherrydale and spending time together as a couple. She couldn't have been more opposed to living without privacy with a missionary family in a squalid ghetto in Calcutta for three weeks, ministering alongside people she barely knew. And to me—as a man with the best of intentions wanting to fulfill God's will for my life—it was unfathomable that my newlywed wife wanted to place our marriage before a mission trip to needy people. However, the lightbulb turned on when I spoke with Pastor Terry, the senior pastor. He reminded me of Deuteronomy 24:5 and the need to prioritize my marriage and have the two of us come together to serve Christ in a mutually agreeable manner."

"You are right, Pastor," Deacon Fullam said. "We need to focus our answer to this man in love, for he may be convinced that he is serving God and his family best in his present course of action."

Stephen and the deacons then bowed their heads and prayed, one after the other, for the man, his wife, and their marriage. Stephen stated that he would carefully meditate on God's Word and seek guidance from Him before advising the man as to how to build up his marriage.

He then opened a second prayer request and shared it with the deacons:

> *Please pray for my son, who has gotten into the wrong crowd at school and is experimenting with drugs. I'm really worried that he is rebelling against everything good in his life, and it's breaking my heart.*
>
> *From: A Very Concerned Mom.*

After they had finished praying for this mother and her son, Stephen spoke about the need to get more teenagers involved in youth groups and team mission trips to the inner city and elsewhere.

"We need to engage our youth as servants of Christ, showing them that the Word is alive. It is a powerful seed that can reap a bountiful harvest in themselves and others," he said.

"Amen," Deacon Peralta pronounced, sharing Pastor Stephen's sentiment.

"Allow me to share with you one example of the harvest that such service can produce," Stephen continued. "When Brian was in eighth grade, Laura and I encouraged him to become a 'big brother' to an inner-city boy from a broken home in Washington, D.C. Each week, Brian helped this young boy named Rudy with his homework and spent time listening as Rudy shared his life experiences.

"Soon, Rudy and Brian were praying for one another on a regular basis. Brian invited Rudy to join us at family barbecues and brought him along on our summer bass fishing trips to Shenandoah National Park. Not only did Rudy benefit from this experience—he is a guidance counselor at the same high school from which he graduated six years ago and continues to stay in touch with Brian—but Brian also grew tremendously from this service. Brian learned to focus on the needs of others first and to put his personal concerns and worries into perspective. He also learned to appreciate all of the blessings that God has bestowed on our family."

"I fully agree with you, Pastor Steve," Deacon Lindquist said. "Brian's service to others since the days of his childhood has been exemplary, and his focus on others has made him into an individual we greatly admire and respect. As leaders of our church and members of our community, we need to expand the opportunities for the youth to serve God in real-life experiences."

"There are tremendous needs to fulfill, even in ministering to the youth of our congregation, Pastor Steve," Deacon Frye concurred. Carefully choosing his words, he continued, "I know that Brian volunteered to serve as youth pastor earlier this year but has been unable to attend teen programs as often as he would like. Do you think we need a second youth pastor to fill in for Brian from time to time, especially with his getting married and all?"

"Yes, I've been thinking about that," Stephen responded, keeping his voice calm. "I propose that we advertise the need for a second youth pastor in our service this Sunday."

The deacons nodded their assent to the pastor's proposal.

Steve nodded back, pleased that they had agreed to this without the need for further deliberation. "All right now, there appears to be one remaining prayer request in the prayer box. Let's consider it together, and then we can adjourn."

Stephen placed his hand into the cardboard box and retrieved a crumpled-up piece of paper. Opening it, he saw that it was written in a child's hand. With some difficulty, Stephen made out the words, despite several misspellings, and read them aloud:

Dear church, please pray for my kid bruther Joey. The doctor told my mom and dad yesterday that Joey has lukemea. Joey is only four years old and is a real nice bruther. I play baseball with him in our backyard. I'm scard that Joey will get sick or die. My mom tells me that Jesus really luvs us kids. She says He takes some sick kids home to Heaven and makes them better there before they grow up. Joey is a real good kid and I want him to be here on earth until he gets real old. Please pray that God makes Joey better soon so his lukemea goes away and he can stay with me and mom. Last week, I prayd for a new baseball gluv; but if God is two busy to anser both prayers, I want God to make Joey better. Paster Steev, please remind God how special . . .

Stephen's voice became softer and softer until it trailed off into inaudibility. An awkward silence followed.

"Pastor Steve, are you all right?" Deacon Peralta finally asked, gazing up at the pastor.

The deacons were startled to see that Stephen's eyes were closed and a tear was streaming down his face.

"Please . . . excuse me for a moment," he said, rising to his feet and quietly leaving the room.

It was not unusual for Pastor Steve to express heartfelt concern and empathy for the welfare of his congregation, but rarely had they witnessed him so visibly moved by a prayer request.

"Do you think this has anything to do with Brian?" Deacon Frye asked with concern.

"It may. It may have a lot to do with Brian, I'm afraid," Deacon Peralta answered.

They held hands and quietly prayed for Brian before the pastor, now composed and bearing a reassuring smile, re-entered the room. Without explaining the reason for his recent emotion, Pastor Steve joined them in a prayer for Joey, Joey's younger brother, and both of their parents.

Having concluded their prayer meeting, the deacons congratulated Stephen once more on Brian's wedding. Then, in a pensive silence, they respectfully took their leave.

CHAPTER 9

John drilled the eight ball into the far corner pocket with precision, ending the game with four striped balls sitting on the table.

"You'd think Brian and I were pool hustlers—like Newman and Cruise in *The Color of Money*. We should take our show to the officer's club, Bri."

"Yeah, we're the perfect team, John. I lull our opponents into thinking that we're as green as a dollar bill, and you clear the table like Cruise's character, Vince Lauria," Brian responded. "Let's sit down and grab a bite to eat, gentlemen, and then we'll get our show on the road."

Brian and his four groomsmen sat at a booth and ordered generous amounts of buffalo wings, Swedish meatballs, chilled shrimp, and Edgar's famous crab cakes to top it all off.

"You're going to need to put some skin on those bones just in case your missus' cooking leaves something to be desired," Ron kidded. "This could be your last decent meal in a long time, aside from the wedding food—which you'll have but a few minutes to savor between pictures and going table-to-table to greet your well-fed guests."

"You sound like a man in the know," John stated with a wry smile. "How many years have you been married?"

"One too many," Ron replied with a good-natured laugh.

"Me, too," quick-witted John promptly rejoined.

"This meal should provide me with more than enough reserves to last the entire day," Brian stated. "It may not be wedding food, but it'll be tastier than the MREs out in the field; although, come to think of it, I did take a liking to the chow mein noodles in the beef teriyaki MRE."

"I'm still partial to the Country Captain Chicken with mashed potatoes," John offered. "Though Afghan shish kebab with steaming naan and raisin-topped rice is top shelf and my favorite from the locals' menus."

"So, besides preparing to be Mrs. Johnson, tell us a little about what the lucky bride is up to these days, Brian," Gabe prodded.

"Sure. As a couple of you already know, Beth is working as an RN at Johns Hopkins and really likes it so far. She's been there almost two years, less the month she took off after I returned to the States."

"That's great that she took a month off to be with you when you came back," Gabe responded. "From everything you've told me, it sounds like she's really been there for you."

"Definitely. She was by my side, brightening every laborious day of my rehabilitation with her encouragement and joyful spirit. It really kept my morale up during some very challenging days at Walter Reed . . . especially while I was processing some survivor's guilt—thinking about why I deserved to pull through while some of my brother warriors—great men, with families—never made it back."

"It's all right, man," John said instinctively. "You saved a lot of lives, including those of men who wouldn't otherwise have come home alive without your sacrifice that day."

Brian nodded and said softly, "Thanks, John."

"Yeah, I don't think we should look at it from the angle of trying to figure out who deserved to live and who didn't," Gabe said, offering his thoughts. "And I'm sure you don't do that with your patients, either. The only thing we can do is thank God and live every day of life he gives us to the fullest."

"Amen to that," Brian said with a smile. "I'm very blessed that God gave me the skills to serve as a medical officer in combat and equally blessed to have met Beth.

She's one of the most selfless individuals I've ever met, and that's saying something, given my present company."

"Well . . ." John began, and then, for a rare moment, found himself unsure as to what to say.

"I wholeheartedly agree. You and Beth are each blessed in that regard, then," Gabe said, breaking the awkward silence. "As a friend who has gotten to spend quality time with both of you since your return from Landstuhl, I have seen each of you actively seek out opportunities to help others time and again. Unfortunately, that is sometimes a rare thing outside of the military and the medical field these days. No offense intended to your congressman, Paul."

"None taken," Paul replied. "You're right. That quality is rare these days, including on Capitol Hill—aside from my congressman, of course."

"We Americans traditionally view our own representative as the single exception to the rule that politicians are corrupt and self-serving," Brian observed. "What's your sense of Congress' commitment to the war on terrorism, Paul?"

"Unfortunately, each party in Congress is currently mired in a partisan battle to blame the other for September 11," Paul answered. "The 9-11 Commission has a historic task before it and needs to focus on improving our nation's security for the future, rather than blaming people for the mistakes of the past. Accountability is important, but the truth is that neither party—and few people in our government—recognized what kind of war we were in prior to September 11. But I'm optimistic, and I seriously believe that at their core, nearly everyone in Congress is committed to winning the war on terrorism—though they may have different views on how to accomplish that."

"That's good to hear," Brian replied. "Because sometimes people don't realize how much their support and our leaders' commitment to winning the war means to the men and women fighting out there on the frontlines. I mean, no one wants to sacrifice their life for a cause that their nation does not believe in."

"Agree with you one hundred percent," Gabe said. "And I believe that Americans today support our troops more than at any time since World War II. We have people and airlines donating miles to fly us back home to visit our families, thousands of Americans sending us care packages and supporting the families of fallen soldiers, and fellow countrymen giving returning troops standing ovations at airports as they return from duty. I can't tell you how much it meant to me personally to be treated like a hero when I finally came home. My hometown—a town of only three thousand people outside of Fort Worth—had a parade in my honor, and my high school even named its gymnasium after me when I finally returned last spring. Coming home to that level of appreciation was one of the most gratifying experiences of my life."

"That's powerful stuff," John said. "And indeed, you are a hero, Gabe. You volunteered for one of the most terrifying missions in Operation Enduring Freedom: risking your life in enemy-held territory to locate a missing American, all the while not knowing whether you were on a rescue or recovery mission. That uncertainty did not cause you to waver from—or give up on—your mission, which you continued for as long as you were physically able—until that misdirected Hellfire missile knocked you unconscious. You are, in my book, one deservedly distinguished American hero. Let's toast to another hometown hero!"

"Here's to Gabe, an amazing warrior and even better friend!" Brian said, raising his glass in sincere tribute.

"Here's to Gabe!" the others echoed, toasting their sodas and ice waters to the Delta Force sergeant.

"You guys are too much," Gabe said, slightly embarrassed by the attention. "And you're misdirecting the spotlight. Here's to the real hero, the groom!"

They each clanged glasses once again in hearty toasts to Brian. Then, to Brian's relief, the waiter brought over their food before the toasts had a chance to fully devolve into roasts.

"Bri, are you still working in the ER at Harford Memorial Hospital?" Ron asked while helping himself to a couple of steaming hot crab cakes.

"I stopped a couple of months ago. There was just a lot going on, including helping to put this wedding together."

"I can imagine," Ron replied. "Are you planning on going back there to work after the wedding?"

"Probably not during the honeymoon," Brian kidded. "I'm considering a few things. We'll see."

"Heard you're up at Boston University Med School," John said to Ron, changing the subject.

"Yeah, I'm finishing up my second year. I'll be taking my boards in a few months."

"That's your first set, and then you take a second set of boards after your fourth year, right?" John asked.

"That's right," Ron answered. "And then, hopefully, I'll begin my residency, eventually specializing in orthopedic surgery."

"That's great. What makes you lean toward that specialization versus another?" John asked.

"Well, my brother, Gary, is a doctor—an oncologist with his own successful practice. So, I was considering joining him and doing surgical oncology for a while. Then he told me about an experience he had during his oncology residency at Columbia Presbyterian that led me to rethink everything."

"What was that?" John prompted.

"Well, apparently, Gary and several other doctors and nurses took a liking to one of their patients—a really humorous, upbeat guy named Robert, if I remember correctly. Robert was in his late thirties and had a wife who was just entering into the ninth month of her pregnancy. Unfortunately, Robert had an advanced case of non-Hodgkin's lymphoma, which, as you know, is a type of cancer of the lymph nodes. He was scheduled to undergo six cycles of chemotherapy. Shortly after he successfully completed his first cycle of chemotherapy, his wife gave birth to a healthy baby boy.

"My brother and the other doctors and nurses were so happy for Robert that an hour after delivery, they wheeled his wife into his hospital room and brought the baby straight over to him for a surprise celebration, complete with party streamers and cake. Later that evening, my brother even smoked a cigar with Robert in honor of the occasion—which, of course, strictly speaking, was not allowed at the hospital. Gary told me that Robert was in great spirits and talked about going home as soon as possible to spend time with his wife and newborn son.

"Two days later, Robert passed away from the cancer. My brother and everyone else at the hospital who knew Gary were devastated. Apparently, the head of oncology at Columbia Presbyterian found out about what had happened and warned my brother's oncology team against ever becoming so attached to a patient again. And so, Gary detaches himself emotionally from his patients as much as possible these days, heeding that instruction and keeping that 'lesson' in the back of his mind. I couldn't do that, and even if I could, I wouldn't want to have to do that each day in my practice. So, my intention is to specialize in orthopedics: repairing shoulder and knee injuries, doing hip replacements, and the like."

Ron's intense medical account abruptly took Brian back to his first day at Landstuhl following his seven-hour emergency airlift by C-141 cargo plane to Ramstein Air Base.

Brian could hear the wailing of sirens as an ambulance sped through the streets of Landstuhl toward the largest American medical facility overseas. Staring upright at the cold, steel ceiling of the ambulance, he felt helpless and uncertain.

At the facility, Brian was hastily transported to the Deployment Warrior Medical Management Center, where he was immediately whisked into an x-ray room. There, a radiologist x-rayed areas of his neck, face, and lower legs. Brian then waited twenty excruciatingly long minutes in a hospital bed until the radiologist returned to inform Brian of the results.

The bad news was that Brian had a fractured tibia, which required immediate surgery in order to remove shrapnel and dead tissue from the wounded area. This surgery would allow the wound to be properly cleaned and treated with antibiotics and anti-tetanic serum. The good news was that Brian's wounds to his neck and face were more superficial. Their treatment required a less invasive surgical procedure than the one to remove the shrapnel from his leg; a similar cleaning, with antibiotics and a tetanus serum treatment, would follow.

The radiologist went on to explain that an external fixator—a sort of sophisticated bar and clamp mechanism—would then be attached to Brian's tibia in order to correct the dislocated fragments and properly align the tibia for healing. Brian's mind was overloaded with information, and he absorbed only a fraction of what the radiologist proceeded to inform him regarding the surgeries and treatments needed in order to reconstruct his soft tissue and tibial bone defects.

At this point, Brian recalled feeling more stressed and overwhelmed than he had on the field of battle during the rescue operation when a combination of adrenaline, instinct, training, and the urgency of the mission at hand led him to take decisive action before his mind could fully apprehend the dangers or consequences of his actions. Although the doctors and nurses at the hospital were well-trained, professional, and well-intentioned, it was not they who did the most to restore Brian's morale or to instill in him the drive and self-discipline to heal as completely and speedily as possible under the circumstances. Rather, it was the men and women in uniform lying beside him who brought him the most inspiration. These fellow Purple Heart-recipients shared their amazing stories of heroism and sacrifice with him, brightening his darkest days. Each waking hour of each day, they struggled together, as military family, to emotionally and physically heal and rehabilitate.

It was men like Gabe Sheffield, Brian presently thought to himself, *and men like those marines who shared the hospital bay at Landstuhl with me.* Brian immediately recounted what a marine commandant and other fellow wounded marines had done at Landstuhl for a gravely injured marine. The marine had suffered IED-induced burns to more than seventy percent of his body and related combat injuries that rendered him a paraplegic for life.

It was the afternoon of Ben's birthday. Over a dozen marines all gathered together in the bay in which Ben lay. Some walked in; others wheeled themselves in; and one was even required to be carried into the room on a stretcher. Regardless of how they had entered, each marine carried an American flag. Ben's face lit up with each marine who entered, and he gave a big thumbs up as the commandant approached his hospital bed.

In response, the commandant crisply saluted Ben, prompting Ben to return the salute. The commandant bore a ceremonial sword and a Bible. He opened his Bible to a tabbed page and began to read Psalm 23 from the beginning. "The Lord is my shepherd; I shall not want . . ."

One by one, each man and woman in the room, including Ben and Brian, joined the commandant in reciting King David's most treasured psalm. As soon as they concluded, the commandant signaled for an attendant waiting just outside the bay to wheel in a huge birthday cake on a cart. Ben's eyes lit up, reflecting the warmth of the candles and the people around him, as the cart was whisked into the room.

"Ben, in addition to blowing out the candles and making a wish, I'm going to ask you to cut the cake with this sword. This sword—and not the cake, mind you—has been passed down in my family for four generations from one marine to the next," the commandant said, injecting a bit of humor.

As the commandant guided Ben's paralyzed hand in cutting the cake, the marines spontaneously cried out, "Semper fi," nearly in unison. Brian saw Ben's face, scarred with third-degree burns, tear-streaked with emotion. It was an occasion that Brian would never forget.

Pivoting back to the present, Brian collected his thoughts and cleared his throat, composing emotions that might otherwise swell to the surface. "Well, personally, I think your brother did the right thing, Ron. Medicine has a human face on both the doctor and the patient side, and we need to remember that. There's more to the healing process than just physical treatment, and . . . Cancer can be an especially unpredictable beast," he added without elaboration. "So, guys, where do you think Sweetney will go in the NBA draft?" Brian asked, abruptly changing topics to a lighter one.

The question ignited a spirited debate over whether or not Mike Sweetney of the Georgetown Hoyas would be selected with one of the top ten picks in the upcoming draft. With the animated debate having concluded by a narrow three-to-two margin that Sweetney would indeed crack the top ten, Brian and the groomsmen headed out to Maryvale Castle for the main event of the day.

CHAPTER 10

A s the wedding photographer approached Maryvale Castle, she was struck by the stately beauty of the turreted stone manor, modeled after Warwick Castle. To Jacquelyn's mind, the meticulously maintained, emerald-green grounds compared favorably with those of its more famous English counterpart. As she drove past the front entrance and into the parking area, an elderly woman, garbed in the traditional black habit of a nun, peered out at her from a second-story window.

She must be one of the sisters of Notre Dame de Namur, Jacquelyn surmised. She recalled that the proprietor of the sprawling, Tudor-style manor was reputed to have sold it to this order of nuns back in 1945, giving rise to the founding of Maryvale Trinity College Preparatory School.

During much of the day, the Great Hall of the castle served as a lecture hall for its students, while other areas within the castle housed a chapel, a library, administrative offices, and classrooms. Nearly every Friday, Saturday, and Sunday during the spring, summer, and fall, the castle provided a historic site for weddings, engagement parties, dances, reunions, and other special events.

As Jacquelyn made her way toward the front entrance, she appreciated the elegant chamber music emanating from a stone building, which once served as Maryvale's carriage house.

Sounds like one of Schubert's string quartets, she thought, reminiscing back to her days playing the violin in the Maryland Classic Youth Orchestra. *Not bad—in a few years, they might even be able to walk across the way and play at a Maryvale wedding.*

Brian and Beth had informed Jacquelyn that a classical string quartet would, in fact, play as a prelude to their wedding ceremony and during the ensuing dinner. Beth's aunt, a high-end interior designer with an array of socialite connections, had booked an internationally renowned quartet for the ceremony. The Crystal Strings, who had played at Rockefeller family weddings and the Barcelona Summer Olympics, would entertain their wedding guests with a dazzling repertoire of Haydn, Mozart, Beethoven, and Schubert. Beth had specifically requested that Jacquelyn take some wedding photos of the tuxedo-clad quartet, knowing they would add a refined backdrop to the wedding.

As Jacquelyn walked into the main entrance of the castle, she saw a florist taking direction from a middle-aged woman clad in a high-end, red suit.

"Please arrange the centerpieces just like this," the woman instructed, gesturing to a stunning arrangement of roses, lilies, asters, and chrysanthemums accented with greenery.

"That's really beautiful," Jacquelyn commented.

The woman immediately turned around and smiled. "Why, thank you, dear. I'm Beth's aunt, Cleo. I have the honor and tall task of being the wedding coordinator. You must be Jacquelyn."

"My camera gives me away every time," Jacquelyn said, smiling.

"Beth so raved about your work that I had to see it and judge for myself. After viewing your demo album of General Cox's wedding, I came away a big fan."

"Why, I'm flattered. Thanks so much, Mrs.—"

"Please, just call me Aunt Cleo. Your family just got a lot larger today, dear," she said, placing a hand on Jacquelyn's back in a welcoming manner. "Now, I've noticed, Jacquelyn, that quite a bit of your photography is of military weddings and ceremonies. What piqued your interest in that subject?"

"Why yes, I'm a military brat, so to speak. I was born at Ramstein Air Base in Germany—the daughter of an air force colonel. Having moved from country to country following my father's career across Europe and eventually back to the States, I've both loved and hated aspects of military life. But I've always admired the men and women who serve."

"Why you're the perfect person for this wedding, then. We're all so proud of Brian and what he's done for his country."

"Understandably so. You see, I'm well aware of Brian's service. As a photographer for *Stars and Stripes,* I covered the ceremony in which Brian was awarded the Silver Star, and I also photographed his arrival back home. It's not a coincidence that I'm here today for the wedding, Aunt Cleo. I was set to fly to London for a family vacation this week until Beth approached me two months ago, telling me how much she and Brian wanted me to be a part of this wedding and how much it meant to them. She poured out her heart about their continued mission to help heal the undeserved through their medical and spiritual gifts. They're an extraordinary couple, and I could not refuse.

With all we've shared over the past couple of months, we've become good friends. That's why I'm so excited to be here today."

"Why, bless your heart," Aunt Cleo said as she gave Jacquelyn an impromptu hug. "They are such a special couple, and we are all going to make this wedding wonderful for them. Darling, let me take you around to introduce you to the head caterer and the florist. The baker should be arriving any minute with the wedding cake, and in about half an hour, the ice sculptor is set to deliver the ice sculpture for the wedding table centerpiece."

"How elegant," Jacquelyn remarked. "What will the sculpture look like?"

"It consists of two interlocked hearts mounted on a floral ice arrangement. We have special lighting and some real flowers to highlight the sculpture and radiate its beauty throughout the room. It's a surprise gift from Stephen's congregation. I think Brian and Beth will absolutely love it."

"That'll be lovely and should photograph very well for the wedding album," Jacquelyn commented.

Aunt Cleo proceeded to introduce Jacquelyn to the head caterer and the florist, each of whom was immersed in pre-wedding preparations and took but polite notice of the young woman.

"Let me show you the wonderful landscape out back," Aunt Cleo said. "The rose gardens are gorgeous, and the forested meadow backdrop is absolutely spectacular."

Within the span of half an hour, Jacquelyn visualized a myriad of photos that she would take: pictures of the bride and groom kissing on the crest of the hill overlooking the forest; sauntering in the rose garden; posing behind the ice sculpture; laughing before the string quartet; descending arm-in-arm down the winding central stairwell; cutting the multi-tiered, rose-petal wedding cake; being toasted by the best man and matron of honor in the Great Hall; exchanging vows on the stately terrace overlooking the back lawn; and embracing before the warmth of the hearth's fire. Of course, she recognized that many of the most special photographs would be those that captured a spontaneous moment, immortalizing a genuine action or emotion without awareness or pretense. The trick was for her to be situated in the right location at the right time to capture the subjects amidst the perfect lighting, setting, and backdrop. This was not an easy task, but rather a formidable challenge, one which Jacquelyn especially looked forward to this day in a wedding that was to prove more memorable than she could ever imagine.

CHAPTER 11

It was now five p.m. Brian stood in uniform at the top of the castle veranda beside his father overlooking 120 guests seated in rows of chairs on the castle lawn below. He had decided to be married in full Ranger uniform replete with his Silver Star and Purple Heart in honor of the men with whom he had served in Afghanistan. Following the ceremony, Brian planned to change into his tuxedo for the dinner reception and related evening festivities.

In memory of those who had fallen, lest they otherwise be forgotten on the most significant day of his life, Brian had hung a framed, folded, American flag in the castle vestibule. It bore the inscription: "In memory of our brothers-in-arms who gave their lives for our country."

Brian's father, Stephen, stood beside him, Bible in hand, as one by one, each groomsman accompanied a bridesmaid to her place on the cascading steps of the veranda before taking his place atop a step opposite her. Not wanting to detract from the attention they felt should rightly be focused on the wedding couple, John and Gabe had each respectfully declined Brian's offer for them to dress in military uniform for the ceremony.

Presently, John escorted Lisa, arm in arm, along a stone walkway and up the stately steps of the veranda. Brian smiled at John as he walked across the terrace before taking his place one step below Brian and his father.

Brian now gazed past the bridesmaids toward the path Beth would momentarily begin to traverse with her father in a special, bittersweet walk toward her married life. It was not bittersweet in the sense that either Beth or her father, Sheldon, had the least bit of reservation about Brian. Rather, both Beth and Sheldon realized that this signified the end of a chapter in their close father-daughter relationship. She had been her daddy's girl from the moment he first held her, and as the younger of Sheldon's two daughters and last to be married, she occupied a special place in his heart.

The bridesmaids looked lovely as they stood, bouquets in hand, with their teal blue dresses gently ruffling in the afternoon breeze; but Brian's mind was focused on one woman—the woman who would, in a matter of minutes, be his wife. He recalled in a sudden flurry of memories the moment he had first met Beth, the moment he had fallen in love with her, and the moment he had proposed to her in a hot air balloon, two thousand feet above Charlottesville, Virginia. He remembered what it was that had led him to fall in love with this remarkable woman in the first place.

A brisk, March wind gusted across the blue-gray waters of the Potomac. As Brian walked by Beth's side along Georgetown's Harbor wharf, she appeared to lose her equilibrium and cried out in pain. Observing her heel caught between two wooden planks, Brian instinctively lent a helping hand. Quickly steadying her, he deftly shifted her weight off the leg of her immobilized foot and then gently freed it. Her balance and serenity regained, she offered Brian an embrace full of affection, which he readily accepted

and returned with a kiss. The demure, brown eyes of the eighteen-year-old sparkled with delight and appreciation.

Since the medical mission trip to Kenya, Brian and Beth had intermittently stayed in touch: first writing and then emailing each other. When Beth, then a prospective George Washington nursing student, found out that Brian would attend Georgetown, she had been elated. And when he had called her during the fall of their freshman year and asked her out to a school play, she had excitedly accepted. Since then, they had regularly dated and now, midway through their spring semester, referred to each other as boyfriend and girlfriend without even batting an eye.

One pleasant Saturday evening, a couple of weeks following the windy change-of-season weather, Brian persuaded Beth to venture with him on another stroll along the harbor. Engrossed in conversation as they walked off a delicious but unhealthy deluxe burger dinner at Clyde's, they made their way down Twenty-third Street, across a park, and onto a wooden promenade overlooking the Potomac.

Brian presently asked Beth what had prompted her to volunteer at the Elizabeth Taylor Medical Center on Fourteenth Street. Her eyes ablaze with passion for the topic, Beth explained her motivation for having done so.

"George Washington offers a Big Sibling program, where you can volunteer to mentor a poor boy or girl from the District. As the baby sister of my family, I thought it was time to change roles and be an older sister to someone who could use an older sibling. So, I enrolled in the program and was matched with Kendra, an adorable eight-year-old girl from a run-down neighborhood in Anacostia.

"For our first outing, I decided to take her to an ice cream parlor to put her at ease and get to know her. While sitting with Kendra at a table eating ice cream, I asked about her family. Kendra informed me that she had a *mommy and a sister—no father—and that both of them were sick. When I asked her what she meant by this, she told me that her mother had AIDS and that her three-year-old sister was born with HIV."*

Brian shook his head in sad disbelief.

"Not only did this poor girl—at age eight—know the words 'AIDS' and 'HIV,' but she also told me that her mommy had instructed her that if she found Mommy very sick or came home one day and did not see Mommy, she must call Grandma and stay at her house. Can you imagine how this broke my heart?" Beth asked.

"Wow, that's just crazy," Brian said. *"What can you say to a kid like that?"*

"I told her that she could always call me and that I would talk to her and be her friend. Think of what will happen to Kendra if her mother—not to mention her little sister—passed away. She has no father. Her grandma loves her but doesn't have the means to care for her. I don't want AIDS to tear families apart and ruin children's lives. I want to make sure that mothers with HIV and AIDS get tested, get treated, and don't run the risk of giving HIV and AIDS to their children. That's why I volunteered to help test and treat people at The Elizabeth Taylor Medical Center, which is part of the Whitman-Walker Clinic."

It was then that Brian fully appreciated that his girlfriend was someone very rare and giving—someone who not only cared about others but actively sought to impact their lives for the better. These were values which, thanks to Brian's parents, he shared—values which would lead him to serve proudly in the military as a Ranger medic. He saw that Beth was most passionate when she spoke about the unmet needs of others. It was at this moment—when Brian realized that Beth's inner beauty exceeded her outer beauty—that he fell in love with her.

The quartet began to play the sublime music of Johann Pachelbel's "Canon in D" as Beth, accompanied by her father, came into view and began to proceed toward Brian.

She looks breathtaking, Brian thought as he watched her, staggered by her dignified resplendence and the love he felt for her.

Beth looked joyous and radiant wearing a delicate, yet sophisticated, white wedding dress, a flowing veil, a pearl necklace, and an intricately woven bracelet that reminded Brian of the stunning jewelry he had presented her so many years ago overlooking the savannah. Her brilliantly beaded bracelet elicited murmurs of admiration as she proceeded along the stone pathway and approached the steps of the veranda. Beth's father escorted her without displaying outward emotion, even though he was torn by simultaneous feelings of joy and sadness. As she approached the steps, Brian descended, proudly shook hands with Sheldon, and re-ascended the stairs arm in arm with his resplendent bride.

Looking at Beth, Brian saw a face full of joy and elation. Her smile radiated warmth, passion, and excitement—the very qualities that had attracted Brian to her from the moment they had first met in Kenya. Knowing Beth as well as he did, Brian detected a bit of nervous anticipation in her eyes. He knew how meaningful this ceremony was to her. She had taken everything to heart, not leaving any detail to chance. Together, she and Brian had planned everything about this day in order for it to be one of the most special and memorable days of their lives—everything, that is, but one speech, which Brian was to deliver. In some ways, this speech was too personal for him to share in advance, even with her—his best friend, soon-to-be wife, and confidante.

Scanning the guests gathered before them, Brian fixated on the faces of the men and women who had shaped his life—friends and members of his family who had shared critical stages of his journey, helping to forge his character and the principles that defined his very essence.

Looking at his father, he could hear the words that had echoed in his mind since the day of his faith-confirming baptism twelve years ago. *"Son, to whom much is given, much is expected. Use the gifts your Heavenly Father has given you to serve God, your country, and your community and above all, helping those who are helpless, defending those who are defenseless, and inspiring those who are without hope to live an abundant life."*

Brian looked out at his grandfather, Raymond Johnson, and understood what people meant when they referred to those who served in World War II as "the greatest generation." He saw a man who, in a matter of months, had matured from a sweet, Pennsylvania farm boy into a combat veteran, who shed his blood on the beaches of Normandy. This was the man who had inspired him to become an Army Ranger.

He saw his mother, a good-hearted woman who always shared life's blessings with others and had encouraged Brian throughout his life to do the same. She had motivated Brian from an early age to better his community and assist those less fortunate who existed in a harsher reality outside of the comparatively sheltered world into which he had been born. The civic consciousness she had instilled in Brian had led him to join the Boy Scouts, volunteer to build homes alongside poverty-stricken families with Habitat for Humanity, coach track events for the Maryland Special Olympics, and spend Saturday mornings during his eighth-grade year tutoring and befriending an inner-city boy named Rudy.

Rudy was a testament to the principle that a positively impacted life betters the lives of countless others who later interact with that individual. At the tender age of thirteen, Rudy had quit his gang, refocused his life, and hit the books. As a result, he had graduated from high school with honors. As the first in his family to even graduate from high school, let alone attend college, Rudy had been admitted to the University of Maryland on a partial academic scholarship and had gone on to excel there. Four years later, he graduated from Maryland with high honors and a Bachelor of Arts degree in psychology. Instead of applying for more lucrative, big-city jobs, Rudy chose to pay it forward. He did this by counseling inner-city youth to stay clear of gangs and drugs and to set ambitious life goals for themselves.

Rudy found it especially rewarding to infuse young boys and girls with hope and self-confidence in even the most challenging circumstances. He loved to inspire them by sharing his self-realized adage that the harder a dream is to attain, the more special and worthwhile it becomes. Seeing his fulfilled, African American friend beaming in the glow of his wife, Tina, Brian returned Rudy's toothy smile with one of his own.

Brian next locked eyes on a dark, lustrous face adorned with a rich blue and red beaded necklace beneath a beaming, toothy smile—toothy that is, except for two missing lower central incisors. The guest was clad in a red tunic; beside him stood an exquisitely robed woman—her tender face bejeweled with long hanging earrings and a deep blue necklace. She cried out, *"Esidai!"*—the Maasai word for "beautiful"—as

Beth walked by. Brian was elated that Kimeli had kept his word to attend their wedding in America, gracing their most blessed occasion not only with his presence but with that of his wife, Naserian.

Beside the Maasai couple sat Brian's battalion commander, J.T. Wright, a man whose integrity, courage, and concern for the welfare of his men had prompted Brian to demand those same attributes of himself in serving with his military "family" in Afghanistan. J.T. had recognized Brian's outstanding cognitive and leadership qualities early on and recommended him as the Distinguished Honor Graduate of his Ranger class. Desiring to further these fine qualities, he had selected both Brian and John to attend the National Advanced Leaders Camp. The physical and psychological training the two had received there had proven pivotal to their decisive leadership and sense of purpose on the field of battle. Going beyond their formal commander-student relationship, J.T. had demonstrated a personal interest in Brian's welfare, visiting him upon his arrival at Walter Reed and several times thereafter to check up on his rehabilitation. J.T.'s empathy and personal understanding of what Brian was experiencing with survivor's guilt had been instrumental in Brian's re-connecting to military brothers and sisters at Walter Reed.

He has such a positive, encouraging spirit about him, Brian reflected. *He helped spark my optimism that I could fully recover and return to serve— that is, until the day . . .*

Suddenly, Brian found himself fighting a losing battle to stave off the dark memories that unwelcomingly streamed into his mind— memories filled with fear and a pained awareness of his mortality.

This is not the time, Brian told himself. He had meticulously planned the wedding in his mind, even the emotions he would feel at this moment, standing beside his loving bride on the cusp of being united together for life. But despite Brian's concerted efforts to the contrary, his mind raced back to a day seared deep inside him.

Following an extensive battery of tests, Brian sat physically and emotionally exhausted and at a loss for words beside Beth, this best friend and confidante whom he had been euphoric to propose to one thousand feet above the earth only weeks before. They waited anxiously in a sterile, black-and-white room that painfully mirrored the stark news that awaited them. With hands clasped in breathless silence, they could hear each tick of the wall-mounted clock.

Brian drew no solace from the fact that behind the clock were the offices of Dr. Sanjay R. Singh, the distinguished surgical oncologist who led the Melanoma and Cutaneous Oncology Group at the acclaimed Cancer Center. A biopsy of a subcutaneous growth on Brian's neck earlier that week had ominously confirmed the suspicions of Brian's primary care physician: namely, that the micrographic surgery at Walter Reed had failed to remove all of Brian's skin cancer.

Alarmed, the physician had immediately scheduled Brian to undergo examination and testing at Sidney Kimmel Comprehensive Cancer Center, the only comprehensive cancer center in the state of Maryland. Thus, Brian had spent the last four hours of his day meeting with Dr. Singh and members of his team, undergoing a detailed physical examination, followed by a barrage of medical tests and procedures. These had included a neck and shoulder biopsy, blood and liver function tests, a radiograph, and a CT scan of his chest.

"Dr. Singh is ready to see you," the assistant finally announced in a voice that sounded bereft of emotion.

Brian hesitated for a moment before rising to his feet and heading toward Dr. Singh's office.

"Brian, wait a second; I'm coming with you," Beth said, as she quickly rose and followed him.

Brian nodded resignedly, feeling intensely private but realizing it was important for her to be there.

"Please, take a seat," Dr. Singh said, gesturing for Brian and Beth to be seated before his enormous, mahogany desk. Brian felt detached from his surroundings and uncomforted by the glossy reports, research papers, and newly released medical journal publications that lay strewn across the desk's massive face. Despite feigning a smile, Dr. Singh himself appeared tense and somewhat uncomfortable.

He cleared his throat and then looked directly at Brian. "I will be frank and upfront with you. Unfortunately, your melanoma has metastasized—that is, spread—beyond the primary tumor in your neck both regionally into your shoulder area as well as to your left lung. While surgical resection of the primary tumor is possible—and, indeed, recommended—it is more difficult to treat the two tumors on your left lung. There are a number of treatment options, but they are essentially palliative in nature, meaning that they may shrink the size of your lung tumors but are unlikely to completely eradicate them. Given that your melanoma is categorized as stage IV—the most serious category due to its metastasis to a distant site beyond its primary site in your neck—your prognosis is poor."

"What does that mean? Are you saying that I'm going to die?" Brian asked incredulously. As a Ranger medic, Brian had been well-trained in treating acute combat injuries on the field of battle. However, evaluating a cancer prognosis, let alone his own cancer prognosis, was beyond anything he had ever been taught; and he felt frustratingly ignorant and helpless.

"I'm not saying that—only that you will need to respond well to combination chemotherapy or immunotherapy in order to have a better prognosis."

"I'm still not following you exactly," Brian said with an edge of confrontation in his voice. "What happens to the average person in my shoes? Am I going to make it?"

Dr. Singh's jawline tightened. Though he looked straight at Brian, he seemed detached, as if he were reporting laboratory results to a fellow researcher. "Without positive response to aggressive treatment, in my best clinical judgment, you will have another six to eight months. Now, if you respond well to such treatment—"

"Six to eight months," Brian repeated aloud, his mind struggling to absorb the gravity of the situation.

Beth, who had closed her eyes in disbelief from the outset, now abruptly dropped her head. Placing her left hand over her eyes, she sobbed softly, unable to control her emotions. Observing this, Dr. Singh gently handed Beth the box of tissues on his desk.

The oncologist had witnessed these reactions too many times before. Although patients and their families had displayed a wide array of emotions over the course of Dr. Singh's career, their most common initial response was denial, followed by anger, sadness, and resignation when they processed that this was actually happening to them or their loved ones. The typical patient aggressively questioned the doctor, hoping against hope that he or she was just a question away from hearing the good news that would somehow miraculously override all of the negative news he or she had just heard. Unfortunately, in this case, the oncology director had no miracle cure to propose to Brian.

"Dacarbazine—or DTIC—is the most widely used chemotherapeutic agent, and the average response to it is three to six months," Dr. Singh continued after a respectful pause. "However, it results in complete *remissions in less than five percent of all patients. Now, there are a number of combination drug therapies that have recently been developed which have proven more effective. The combination of DTIC, carmustine, cisplatin, and tamoxifen has led to approximately a 50 percent response rate in previously untreated patients and produced a complete response rate of approximately 15 percent. The median survival time for responders to such therapy is nearly eleven months. There are also radiotherapy and immunotherapy options . . . "*

Brian's mind stopped processing what Dr. Singh was telling him. He had heard that he was going to die and that it was just a matter of time—mere months—from today. In less than six weeks, he was to be married to the woman sitting next to him—a wonderful, warm, caring woman—and his best friend—whose trembling head lay bowed in her hands, her face covered with tears. No, this could not be happening to him, not at this juncture in his life. He had too much to live for, too much to do, too many people who depended on him—

Brian paused for a moment, as it dawned on him that countless others in his situation must harbor the exact same thoughts. He realized that their worries, fears, and feelings of helplessness were no less valid than his were, bringing a refreshing feeling of connectedness to all those who were experiencing what he was.

★ ★ ★

"Brian," Beth whispered to her groom. "Brian . . ."

Finally catching Brian's attention, Beth's eyes flashed to him that the ceremony was about to commence. Brian apologetically gave her a reassuring smile as he, with every ounce of resolve he had, refocused on the ceremony at hand.

CHAPTER 12

Brian's father proceeded to address the expectant gathering in a resonant pastoral voice. "Dearly beloved, we are gathered here today to join in holy matrimony Beth Anne McKenzie and Brian Raymond Johnson. I find myself tremendously privileged to have been asked to preside over their ceremony here today. As Brian's father, I have been blessed by God to have raised a son with a sound moral compass by which he has navigated through the calms and storms of his life to date. As the soon-to-be father-in-law of Beth, I have been equally blessed to have come to know a woman of deep compassion for others. In counseling them in preparation for their marriage, I have been moved by the depth of their love for each other, by their concern and devotion to the other's well-being, and by their abiding faith in a good and just God Who cares for and watches over them.

"Beth and Brian," Stephen continued, "in preparation for your marriage, I asked each of you to reflect separately on the qualities that you most enjoy and cherish in the other. Neither of you has seen what the other wrote in this regard, and I would like to share with you, and those gathered here today, some of the qualities that your better halves each cited.

"Brian, you said that you are astounded by the selflessness of Beth's love for you and for others. You said that her energy is contagious, energizing you to love and care for others. You said that her passion and devotion to healing and helping the least fortunate among us resonates with your heart. You said the depth of Beth's love for you causes you to be able to love and accept yourself more completely. You said that she nursed your spirit and reaffirmed that it was part of God's plan that you survived the battlefields on which you fought. Lastly, you said that she validates the core of who you are as a person."

Brian felt Beth squeeze his hand, and gazing into her eyes, he could see that she was fighting back tears. Brian was truly staggered by the breadth of her blessing on his life. He sensed that her love for him had only strengthened in the face of potentially losing him. He recalled the moment when he had opened his very soul to her and questioned whether they should still get married.

Beth had answered without equivocation, "I want to share you with God for as long as He'll let me."

Pastor Johnson presently continued, "Beth, you said that you fell in love with a boy under a hot African sun in the savannah who cared for young boys and girls with wounds and illnesses as if they were his little brothers and sisters—and, in a very real sense, they were. He has matured into a man filled with wisdom beyond his years. You wrote, 'Brian is a man full of conviction and courage, ready to sacrifice for whom and what he holds dear. As much as I would have liked to have kept Brian safe by my side, and however painful it has been, I know that Brian indeed heeded a higher calling and chose rightly. I love that Brian is a man who has always followed his moral principles, choosing to serve God, his community, and our country with honor and humility. I feel humbled and privileged to have been asked to marry not only the man I love most but also a hero to me, his family, his friends, his platoon, and his country.

"Thank you for allowing me to share these wonderful thoughts with the rest of your friends and family gathered here today. I was struck that neither of you focused on the superficial things that you love and admire about each other. Rather, each of you cited the inner beauty that you saw in the other. This illustrates to me that you each possess wisdom beyond your years, for you recognize and cherish in each other qualities that will endure, transcending your lives here on earth.

"Allow me to share with you—our friends and loved ones gathered here today—three keys to a successful marriage. This comes from a man whom God has blessed with the one woman in the world who completes who I am as a person. They are as simple and profound as this: to love and respect one another, to nourish and nurture one another, and to share every aspect of your lives with each other . . . "

Standing before his father and this gathering in affirmation of his love for Beth, Brian felt a sense of contentment and fulfillment to a degree he had never experienced before. A reassuring sense of peace swept over him as he realized more than ever that no matter what might transpire, he and Beth loved one another unconditionally and without reservation. Even beyond their love for one another, Brian understood that he and his wife-to-be shared a mission and commitment to healing others—whether on the battlefield, on the operating table, or at a clinic. This sense of purpose had propelled each of them to choose and pursue their individual careers. It would now unite them in a common goal, a higher purpose than simply serving each other's needs.

And it will help me maintain my focus on serving others at a time when I am most tempted to focus inward and wallow in self-pity, anger, and dejection, Brian thought. For he had witnessed firsthand the anguish which several of his convalescing brothers-in-arms had suffered through failing to reign in these emotions. Armed with this knowledge, Brian was determined not to fall into the same emotional trap.

With his affable, unassuming personality, Brian had befriended a number of fellow soldiers at Walter Reed. He had become especially close to those who had returned from Afghanistan bearing permanent, physical injuries and, in some cases, deep emotional scars.

Rarely had these soldiers second-guessed the utility of their service. More often, they had questioned how they would integrate into family and civilian life. Would their apparent vulnerability shatter the larger-than-life images harbored by their spouses, sons, and daughters? Could they experience the intimacy they had previously known with their spouses, or would they always keep a piece of themselves buried and hidden, lest they be overwhelmed by re-living the war's most traumatic experiences?

Their questions had also often included profound, philosophical ones: could they accept what had happened to them, their comrades, and the unfortunate innocent civilians, who, despite all efforts to minimize collateral damage, inevitably had lost their lives? And could they find the same meaning, sense of belonging, and compelling purpose in the civilian workplace that they had found in their military service?

Most painful of all to several of these comrades was survivor's guilt—the guilt of having survived while others had perished—especially those who had lived, trained, and fought alongside them.

Only after returning from Afghanistan and speaking with several soldiers haunted by this did Brian understand the guilt that had led some Holocaust survivors to commit suicide decades following the deaths of their loved ones in concentration camps.

Brian presently recalled his conversation at Walter Reed with Sergeant First Class Dan McPherson.

Dan had narrowly survived a harrowing blue-on-blue fiasco. The friendly fire incident had unfolded as future President Hamid Karzai and his forces closed in on the Taliban stronghold of Kandahar. As enemy forces approached Karzai's forces, a member of the Green Berets' A-Team 574 called in grid coordinates to a B-52 bombardier using new GPS and satellite phones. Unfortunately, the Green Beret calling in the coordinates had not been versed in the idiosyncrasies of the equipment's readout. As a result, he had mistakenly called for a B-52 to drop a one-ton GB-31 satellite guided bomb on a friendly position.

The result had been devastating, instantly tearing apart three of Karzai's mujahadeen, *vaporizing two of Dan's commanders, and hurtling deadly shrapnel through the air. The shrapnel had lacerated the torso of Green Beret Master Sergeant John Biggs, literally tearing him in two. Meanwhile, Dan, a close friend of John from their two months of service as members of a twelve-man Special Forces A-Team, had only sustained superficial lacerations to his left arm, a broken collarbone, and a ruptured ear drum.*

Enraged by the senseless loss of life, Dan had channeled his aggression into the subsequent firefight with the encroaching Taliban fighters, helping to coordinate a fierce air and ground assault that had destroyed a convoy of Soviet-era BRDM personnel carriers en route to reinforce Kandahar. During the combat, a rocket-propelled grenade from a truck-mounted ZU-23-2

automatic cannon had showered Dan with shrapnel, aggravating his friendly
fire injuries and lacerating his neck and chest. After initial treatment in
theater, Dan had been transported by an Air Force C-130 Hercules transport
aircraft to Landstuhl, where he had undergone emergency surgery. Once his
condition had stabilized, Dan was transported to Walter Reed for further
post-surgical treatment, evaluation, and rehabilitation. There, Dan met First
Lieutenant Brian Johnson.

Brian would never forget Dan's words to him the night before Dan was
released. "Brian, I feel guilty that I survived. Why did I deserve to survive
and John to die? Why am I sitting here today, about to return to my family,
while John's wife is a widow and his son is without his father?"

Brian had, to a lesser degree, struggled with the same wrenching
questions, acknowledging that to his friend.

"Dan, I asked myself very similar things: why did some of my dearest
brothers in arms—good friends, husbands to loving wives, and fathers to
adoring children—perish beside me, even while I tried with every ounce of
strength to save them. It was only when I recalled how the great patriarchs of
the Bible followed God's will in faith and humility, even when it seemed that
God's vision for their lives was unattainable and nearly impossible to fathom,
that things made sense to me. For they endured trials and tribulations far
greater than even those that we have faced, and in following the will of God,
they were rewarded. If you don't mind, with my being a preacher's son and
all, I'd love to share with you, my wounded brother, the stories of Abraham,
Joseph, and Moses."

Moved by Brian's concern for him and by the power of his words, Dan
nodded for him to continue.

"In each of their lives, God tested the faith of these men and molded their
lives for the great things he had planned for them. Childless Abram, whom

God renamed Abraham—meaning 'father of a multitude'—followed God's calling, left the land of his fathers at the age of seventy-five, and traveled through strange and dangerous lands. In doing so, he firmly believed the Lord's promise that one day, he would become the father of a great nation.

"Abraham waited another painstaking twenty-five years before his wife, Sarah, finally gave birth to their only son, Isaac. Abraham loved his son greatly, but he demonstrated his faith in God by willingly and obediently offering Isaac as a burnt offering to the Lord. When God saw Abraham's faith, God sent an angel to stop him from killing Isaac, and He provided a ram for the sacrifice in Isaac's place.

"Joseph was sold into slavery in Egypt by his jealous brothers and suffered unjust imprisonment because he refused to be seduced by Potiphar's wife. In prison, Joseph interpreted the dream of the man who had been Pharaoh's chief cupbearer. Two years later, when the magicians of Pharaoh's court were mystified by the meaning of Pharaoh's dream, the cupbearer told Pharaoh of Joseph's gift. Thus, God gave Joseph the opportunity to interpret Pharaoh's dream, which he faithfully did, warning Pharaoh that seven years of plenty would be followed by seven years of famine throughout the land. In gratitude, Pharaoh made Joseph ruler over all of Egypt.

"Wisely, Joseph used his position to store up sufficient grain to save the Egyptian people, as well as his family, from the famine that ensued. In revealing his identity to his guilt-ridden brothers who had come to Egypt to buy food during the famine, Joseph said to them, 'God sent me before you to preserve you a remnant on earth, and to keep alive for you many survivors.[3]

"After striking down an Egyptian who was beating a Hebrew slave, Moses fled into the Midianite wilderness. There, far from the luxuries of Pharaoh's palace, he hid from the Egyptians for forty years before God appeared to

---

3   Genesis 45:7

him in a burning bush. From the burning bush, God instructed Moses to lead His people out of Egypt. Obediently heeding God's commandment, Moses leveraged his upbringing in Pharaoh's court and strength as a fugitive to confront Pharaoh. Never backing down in the face of many dangers, he triumphantly led the people of Israel out of Egypt, across the Red Sea, through the desert, and to the border of the Promised Land.

"You see, all three of these men of faith had to endure great tests and tribulations in order for God's plan to manifest itself in their lives and the lives of their people. Only in the face of adversity and trials could God's righteous deliverance reward their faith in Him and lead to the freedom, salvation, and prospering of His chosen people.

"God has plans for all of our lives. Whether great or small, He has a personal calling for each of us. We are asked to carry our crosses and follow Him, however difficult that may be and whatever pains and suffering must be endured as a result.

"Jesus said to his disciples in Matthew 10, 'Whoever does not take up his cross and follow me is not worthy of me. Whoever finds his life will lose it, and whoever loses his life for my sake will find it.⁴ We must seek His perfect will for our lives, and He will be with us even in the darkest hours."

Hearing these words, Dan embraced Brian and told him that at long last, he felt peace.

★ ★ ★

Recalling how these words had spoken truth to his wounded and recovered brother, Brian presently felt a sense of peace and renewed purpose as he stood before his bride, his family, and his closest friends. He took a moment in silence to thank God for His plan for his life, whatever that might be. And he vowed to God that

---

4   Matthew 10:38-39

for however long God gave him the gift of life, that he would carry his cross and follow God, wherever that might lead.

"I do," Beth stated with a love that resonated through Brian's heart. He suddenly felt the greatest joy he had ever experienced unleashed within him. The intensity of the emotion nearly caused him to cry and shout out with joy at the same time. Swept up by emotion, Brian passionately kissed his wife before his father had even finished saying, "You may now kiss the bride."

Moments later, all those gathered erupted in enthusiastic applause. Above the applause, Brian heard a woman cry out in a foreign tongue, "*Entubul emputa enkop!*" quickly followed by his friend, Kimeli's joyful translation, "*Multiply and fill the earth!*"

Yes, my friends! Brian thought, moved by the love he felt all around him. *I will savor this moment the rest of my God-given life, however long that may be. May we live our married lives filled with God's joy and the love of our friends and families!* Holding Beth's hand, Brian beamed with happiness as he looked out upon all those gathered there before them in celebration.

CHAPTER 13

B eth was likewise elated, her mind simply seeking to absorb and process her euphoria. Gone for the moment was the unsettling uncertainty that had hovered like a storm cloud over her since Brian's diagnosis—and especially in the days before the wedding, leading her to wonder just how long she and Brian would get to spend as husband and wife together. She had inwardly questioned whether they would even be able to celebrate their first wedding anniversary, let alone have children or share the joys and travails of life together as a couple and a family. Screening out everything but her love for Brian, her mind now focused on the incredible union before God and man that had just combined their flesh into one.

Beth presently recalled the words of Brian's father on their last day of pre-marital counseling. *"Through this Divine transformation, a sacred union will be created, establishing a relationship that is primary, not subservient, to each of you. That is, a relationship will be created where spiritual, emotional, intellectual, and physical needs, wants, and desires must be considered first and foremost before your individual needs, wants, and desires. This union shall be subordinate only to your relationship with Jesus Christ. If you seek above all else to live lives pleasing to Christ, He will strengthen and bless your union, using it as a beacon of hope and joy to help others and glorify Him."*

So immersed in this nuptial revelry were Beth and Brian that they were both somewhat startled to hear Stephen announce in a strong, projecting voice, "Please kindly take your seats. Beth and Brian will greet each of you and dismiss you row by row."

The string quartet filled the air with Handel's inspiring "Allegro Maestoso" from *Water Music* as, one by one, each of the four groomsmen proudly escorted their respective bridesmaids down the stairs. Once each couple had promenaded down the spiral staircase, the newlyweds proceeded along the stone pathway toward the wedding guests. The wedding party formed a kind of funnel between the happy couple and their congratulatory guests, who were situated upon the sprawling backyard lawn of the castle.

As Brian and Beth came to a graceful rest with the piece's conclusion, family members quickly rose from the first row, offering warm greetings and embraces.

First among them were Beth's parents, Sheldon and Janice, who eagerly received Brian.

"Welcome to the family, Son!" Sheldon said, heartily embracing his son-in-law.

Beth's mother, Janice, a tall, slightly built woman, likewise hugged Brian. In a soft voice, she said, "I love both of you so much."

"We love you, too, Mrs. McKenzie," Brian said with a smile.

"Please, Brian, call me Mom."

Brian had enjoyed learning from Beth of her mother's work as a neonatal nurse practitioner at Georgetown University Hospital's Neonatal Intensive Care Unit, where she had worked for four years prior to the birth of her firstborn, Lisa. In particular, Brian had been struck by Beth's account of how her parents had met and how her mother had helped redefine her father's philosophy of treating patients.

Setting the scene, Beth had told Brian that Janice had met Sheldon, a typically overworked and underappreciated medical resident in the third of his five years of orthopedic surgical training at Georgetown Hospital.

Her sweet, easygoing manner had impressed the intense aspiring surgeon, who soon found himself making visits to the Neonatal ICU in his precious downtime. Observing the hands-on personal care and affection which Janice displayed in her work with those tiny, premature babies—many of whom clung precariously to life—Sheldon had discerned a higher purpose in his work, as Beth had relayed to Brian.

Re-evaluating the detachment and aloofness he had been taught to employ in his surgeries, Beth's father now saw each surgery as a privileged opportunity to better a life. In addition, he began to take more of an active interest in connecting with patients both before and after surgeries. By envisioning himself as a future husband and father as well as a surgeon, her father had redefined his concept of success.

A two-year courtship had ensued, Beth had told Brian, resulting in an extremely fulfilling marriage. He had witnessed Beth's eyes light up as she confided in him that she saw her parents' marriage as a model to emulate in their married life one day.

As Brian followed Beth down the line of her family members, he received a firm handshake from the elder statesman of Beth's family, Eamon McKenzie. Though eighty-four years old, Beth's grandfather was as fit as a man twenty years his junior and as impressive in speech as he was in appearance. "We're honored to have you as part of the family, Brian," Eamon said. "Your service makes us proud, young man."

"I'm honored to become part of it, sir, and to follow in the footsteps of men such as yourself who served our country in its greatest time of need."

Eamon had served as a Seabee in the 6th Naval Construction Battalion in World War II. A proud student of his father's work as a design engineer for the historic Hoover Dam, Eamon had graduated from college with a degree in mechanical engineering, gone on to build docks and wharfs along the Pacific seacoast, and then voluntarily enlisted in the navy as a Seabee following the attack on Pearl Harbor. Eamon's battalion had followed the marines ashore in the bloody battle of Guadalcanal with orders to rebuild the critical Henderson Field Airstrip. Despite fierce aerial bombing and sniper fire by the Japanese, the men of the 6th Naval Construction Battalion had completed the airstrip and managed to keep it in almost continuous operation during the war. Thus, Eamon and his battalion had gallantly earned the distinction of becoming the first Seabees to construct under enemy fire.

"God bless you," Eamon replied.

After graciously greeting the rest of Beth's family and being welcomed to it with open arms in return, Brian finally stood before his mother.

More than anyone else in my life, she has believed in me and never stopped believing in me, Brian thought.

"I'm so happy for you, Son," she said, with a trembling embrace. "Now you have two women who love you more than life itself." Looking into Brian's eyes, she whispered, "Keep your faith, my son. Never give up. Never stop believing that, with Him, you can overcome."

Brian took a moment to make sure he did not lose his composure and then promised with a determined smile, "I won't."

As Brian turned, he felt a strong embrace and quick release from his friend, Kimeli, who likewise embraced Beth with unfiltered enthusiasm.

"At last, my friends, I see you both in America, just as I promised," Kimeli said, bursting into a broad smile. "And you are together, just as I hoped and prayed. Please let me introduce you to God's greatest gift: my wife, Naserian."

Naserian bent her head in respectful greeting until Beth wrapped her hands around her and said "*Yeyo, takwenya!*"

To which Naserian warmly responded, "*Iko!*"

"You remembered our greeting!" Kimeli cried out with laughter. "You are a true member of our family! I am full of joy that God has brought us all together once again."

Holding one hand on his wife's shoulder and one on Brian's, Kimeli began to chant a traditional Maasai song and to hop in a circle. Drawn into the moment, Brian joined in, hopping along. Turning to Beth, he was surprised to see her remove both wedding shoes.

A moment later, Brian felt Beth's hand upon his shoulder and heard her laughter as she joined them in their dance. A tear of joy came to Brian's eyes as he realized how meaningful their reunion was. Despite separation by ocean for over a decade, they were now here together at the wedding his friend had long envisaged. Reunited in body and spirit, they danced side by side in the same inspired manner as they had at a joyous Maasai wedding the last time they had seen each other.

Though nothing topped their remarkable reunion with Kimeli, Brian felt a welcome surge of energy each time that he and Beth greeted a close wedding guest friend. At last, after the couple had greeted in warm embrace the last of the wedding guests, Brian's father dismissed them to enjoy hors d'oeuvres and musical entertainment by the Crystal Strings.

CHAPTER 14

The many acts of spontaneous joy in the wedding were captured in the memories of their guests and in classic black and white photographs taken by their friend and official photographer, Jacquelyn. Just as a beam of sunlight began to filter through a cloud above, she snapped a picture of the bride and groom kissing on the crest of a hill overlooking the verdant forest below. As the newlyweds sauntered through a gorgeous rose garden, she patiently tracked them with her camera and expertly captured the moment when Brian clasped Beth's hand and she gazed into his eyes.

Jacquelyn also induced some magic images, requesting that Brian tell Beth a joke before immortalizing the moment when Beth burst into laughter. She likewise caught Brian gallantly steadying his long-trained bride as she descended a hand-carved stone stairwell into meticulously maintained flower gardens.

"That was a wonderful moment you captured," Aunt Cleo said, complimenting Jacquelyn's keen eye and quick camera finger.

"Thank you, Aunt Cleo. They're a joy to photograph, and I couldn't be happier for them."

When the outdoor photography had concluded, a caterer offered Beth and Brian the remaining hors d'oeuvres of fresh scallops wrapped in steaming bacon, garlic shrimp, Thai chicken, and mini filet mignon kabobs.

"This is excellent, my friend. It reminds me of the feast we had at Zard Kammar," John said, referring to the lavish buffet that they and several Ranger officers had enjoyed at the wedding of a local Northern Alliance commander following the fall of Mazar-e-Sharif.

"Thanks, John. Yes, the kabobs they grilled for us and their rich stew of vegetables with freshly baked naan was incredible," Brian said, recalling the sumptuous feast to which the famished Rangers had been treated. "Hopefully you'll also enjoy today's wedding cake as much as you did that many-layered cake that we devoured."

"Yes, we probably should have left a few more pieces than we did for the couple and their guests," John said in good humor.

Helping himself to a steaming garlic shrimp, John continued, "Heed Ron's adage and enjoy this food while you can, for who knows what to expect in your first home-cooked meal."

"Judging from your appetite, Lieutenant, you've eaten one too many MREs," Brian lightly rejoined.

"And you've eaten one too many hospital . . . " John stopped himself in mid-sentence, belatedly realizing the inappropriateness of the remark.

Rather than respond to it, Brian adroitly curtailed further conversation on his health by asking the head caterer, "Should we start to get set up for the wedding party introductions?"

"Yes, it's about that time, sir," he responded. Then, raising his voice, the caterer requested, "Please, everyone who is part of the wedding party, kindly ascend the back stairwell just to the right of the Great Hall. After Brian changes into his evening attire, he will meet you at the top of the stairwell. I'll then send the DJ over to run through how each of you would like the introductions to be made." Turning to John and Lisa, he asked, "In the meantime, would you mind assisting the ring bearer and flower girl to the second floor to await their introductions as well?"

"Of course," John answered as Lisa nodded her assent.

The ring bearer, Tim, was the rambunctious seven-year-old son of John's older brother, a former nuclear submarine engineer now serving as a naval procurement officer. Tim loved being the center of attention. Along those lines, he had—earlier that day—gratuitously entertained all wedding guests present with a series of mischievous facial expressions before finally presenting the wedding rings.

The flower girl was Lisa's four-year-old daughter, Amanda, a shy and adorable girl. Being young and overwhelmed by the wedding, she had mistakenly proceeded into the second row of bemused wedding guests before being escorted by Lisa to her choreographed position on the steps of the veranda.

John and Lisa located the animated ring bearer and reluctant flower girl and impressively managed to persuade them to participate in the wedding party introductions by emphasizing how special and important a role each of them would play.

"Your mom, dad, and all of the guests can't wait for you to be introduced. As the most important kid in the entire wedding, you'll go first and show everyone else how to make their entrance. We all know that you're a great leader, Tim, whom every kid wants to follow. That's why you have the special, top-secret role to help Amanda and make sure she does everything right. We all picked you to be in charge, but don't tell anyone," John coached, employing psychological tactics he honed at Ranger School.

Paired together for sixty days of rigorous training, John and Brian had sustained and motivated each other to persevere and graduate from the intense U.S. Army Ranger School course with, in John's case, the Benjamin Church Leadership Award for outstanding leadership.

In contrast to John's appeal to Tim's ego, Lisa employed motherly tactics that were equally effective. She promised her daughter she could stay up late with the grownups if she behaved well and participated in the pageantry.

Meanwhile, the rest of the wedding party obligingly crossed a small chamber adjoining the Great Hall and leisurely made their way up its back stairwell, admiring the elaborate, hand-carved, oak balustrade along the way. Brian slipped into the small library he had used as a dressing room and, after minor assistance from the caterer optimizing his cummerbund and cufflinks, changed into his wedding tuxedo. He then ascended the back stairwell to join his beaming bride and the rest of the wedding party overlooking the front stairwell that spiraled down to the Great Hall.

The DJ paired the cutest couple, the newly inspired Tim and Amanda, followed by the groomsmen and bridesmaids, arranging them in order of their planned entrance. He practiced pronouncing their names and, where appropriate, military titles.

When all had taken their positions, the DJ asked the wedding party, "Are we all ready to rumble?"

"Are we the undercard fight or the main event?" John joked.

"You're on the undercard tonight, my friend; Tim and Amanda and Monsieur and Madame Johnson are the co-main events," the quick-witted DJ rejoined. Then, in a raised voice addressing the entire gathering, he announced, "Ladies and Gentlemen, it is my pleasure this evening to introduce to you the members of the wedding party, beginning with Timothy Morrison and Amanda Reynolds."

"My name's Tim," Tim curtly corrected.

Tim then matter-of-factly took Amanda by the hand and led her down the stairwell, made two ninety degree turns to face the wedding guests at the half-story platform, and continued to the foot of the stairwell. There, Tim took a gratuitous bow, though in his mind, it was well-deserved. He then stood in place soaking up amused applause as naturally as a sponge absorbs water.

"One day, he will make a great addition to the Pentagon's top brass," John quipped. "He loves the limelight, and he takes credit for everything."

Brian nodded with a smile.

The DJ then proceeded to introduce the rest of the wedding party, whereby each groomsman-bridesmaid pair made their entrance and then stood behind their seats at the wedding table awaiting the introduction of the newlyweds.

"Ready for the big moment?" the DJ finally asked Brian and Beth.

The couple nodded, prompting the DJ to intone in a rich baritone, "Ladies and Gentlemen, I have the honor this evening of introducing to you, for the first time, the distinguished couple—an officer and a lady—Lieutenant and Mrs. Johnson."

The Great Hall erupted in applause as Brian elegantly escorted his beaming bride down the sweeping stairwell, her dress cascading behind her. The applause grew as the couple made their grand entrance down the final stairwell to their guests. A whistle from one of Brian's younger cousins punctuated the event and achieved its goal of inducing a blush from the groom.

As soon as the newlyweds gathered themselves at the foot of the stairwell, they took in a wondrous, dreamlike scene; gathered around them was a celebratory assemblage of friends, family, and colleagues who had supported Beth and Brian throughout the various facets of their lives. In the foreground, surrounded on either side by their respective parents, was a brilliantly illuminated ice sculpture consisting of two interlocked hearts mounted on a bed of roses chiseled in ice. Beyond that were the wedding table and guest tables, decorated with delicate white and blue floral arrangements. The lilies of the valley and blue hydrangeas basked in an eerily romantic mix of candlelight and moonlight streaming in through latticed castle windows.

Finally, descending the stairwell himself, the DJ announced, "The congregation of Columbia's First Baptist Church would like to present to Lieutenant and Mrs. Johnson the Intertwined Hearts Ice Sculpture to symbolize the joining of their lives and hearts as one."

Amazing. What a gift. The coolness of the ice actually feels refreshing, Brian thought as his sea-blue eyes swept across the room, locking in grateful camaraderie with those of the members of his congregation in attendance. From his church, he noted four deacons, three friends with whom he had traveled on mission trips to Kenya and South Africa, several members of his college fellowship group, two teenagers he had mentored as church youth pastor, and, of course, his mother and father.

"Thank you. Thank you all so much for this tremendous gift," Brian said as he soaked in the moment, indelibly etching the treasured scene into his memory.

I'll be sure to remember this whenever the slightest doubt creeps into my mind regarding whether I enjoy their love and support, Brian vowed to himself.

Brian noted the click of Jacquelyn's camera as he and Beth warmly welcomed each congregation member to join them in front of the strikingly illuminated sculpture, where he and Beth extended their personal thanks. Brian and Beth then invited both sets of parents to join them in front of the sculpture, symbolizing their families joined into one. Unobserved by Brian, who was caught up in the moment, Jacquelyn crystallized the evening with a beautiful photo of the wedding couple kissing in the center of the glistening hearts. Moments after Jacquelyn snapped the final picture, the caterer bid Brian and Beth to join the wedding party and take their seats at the head table.

CHAPTER 15

O nce all were seated, the guests directed their attention to the wedding table. Striking a handsome figure, John rose to his feet to deliver the first toast of the evening. He cleared his throat as he took the microphone. "I am truly honored to be here with all of you today as Brian's best man. I'd like to kick off my toast by sharing a few thoughts and memories from times Brian and I spent together.

"We met as freshmen at Georgetown's ROTC training program. On our first day of training, our ROTC instructor asked us whether we had it in us to take the life of an enemy combatant. I was surprised—floored may be more accurate—when Brian, in response, questioned whether an army medic had a duty to save the lives of all those wounded, regardless of whether they were friends or foes.

"I thought to myself, 'This guy isn't tough enough to make it as a soldier. He's a thinker, not a fighter—a naïve idealist who will quickly be disillusioned when he realizes what life in the army is really like.'

"Boy, was I wrong. Brian proved himself to be an extraordinary soldier. Here before you today sits a Purple Heart recipient, who was also awarded the Silver Star: the army's third-highest, combat valor decoration. Here before you today sits an Army Ranger first lieutenant, whom our battalion commander, Commander J.T. Wright—an honored guest with us today—selected as the Distinguished Honor

Graduate of our Ranger class. Here before you today sits the man whom I witnessed on the field of battle in the mountains of Afghanistan voluntarily take action which transformed the battlefield and saved the lives of four downed Rangers. I am speaking of heroic action beyond the call of duty—selfless action at great risk to Brian's life and limb—that he himself proposed, shifting the entire tide of battle.

"Most importantly, here before you today is a good and honorable human being and my best friend. I'd like to share an insight into the extraordinary character of this humble man, who would not, for fear of self-aggrandizement, otherwise share it with you.

"For those who may not know, Brian served as a Ranger medic in my platoon in Afghanistan from November of 2001 until wounded in action in March of 2002 during Operation Anaconda. While on patrol in a village outside of Bagram Air Base a month earlier, a squad of men from my platoon, including Brian and me, came across a group of Afghan children. As soon as the children saw us, they ran over and asked for candy. However, one child lagged behind, hopping slowly on one leg.

"Once this child had made his painstaking way over to us, we learned through our interpreter how the child, whose name was Abdul, had been maimed. Abdul had been shepherding a herd of goats for his family when he came across the infamous PFM-1 'butterfly' mine—an airdropped cluster bomblet shaped like a butterfly. Like many Afghan children, the seven-year-old boy had mistaken the mine for a toy and walked over to retrieve it. The mine exploded, blowing off Abdul's foot.

"Lacking proper medical attention, his wound had turned gangrenous, causing him ultimately to lose his entire leg. Coming from a poor village family, Abdul had not been fitted with a prosthetic or even given a pair of crutches to help make his way about.

"Brian not only ensured that Abdul received a prosthetic leg from our medical facilities at Bagram Air Base, but he also persuaded the village's elders to educate the children about the dangers of the 'butterfly' mine. This was quite a feat given the prevailing cavalier attitude Afghans typically exhibit toward land mines.

"Brian's concern about the dangers of land mines has not been confined to his days in theater. Since Brian's return to the U.S., he has become actively involved with Save the Children, USA, a venerable charity that provides mine risk training for sponsors of educational landmine programs around the world. In short, Brian has proven a fine soldier and humanitarian.

"On a more personal note, Brian has proven a steadfast and uplifting friend throughout the years. He is an optimistic person with the courage, vision, and conviction to make good things happen in his life and in the lives of those fortunate enough to be around him. He is a principled man of exceptional character and integrity, whose decisions are led by a sound moral compass—and I am not one to bestow such accolades lightly.

"Standing before you today, I am not only honored to give this toast, but also elated to do so. For Brian has once again exercised excellent judgment in marrying Beth. Beth, as many of you already know, is a wonderful, beautiful, bright, and good-hearted woman. I have no doubt that Brian and Beth will bring great blessings to each other in their marriage.

"So, that being said, I would like to propose a toast to a most wondrous couple. Brian and Beth, may you continue to bring great love and joy to each other, to your friends and family, and to all those who have the privilege of knowing you."

"Here, here" echoed throughout the room as the guests clanged their champagne flutes together in tribute to the newlywed couple. Brian rose to his feet and embraced his "brother," feeling extraordinarily honored and lucky to have him as his friend.

Following the celebration of John's toast, Lisa stood, smiled for a moment, and then began. "Besides Beth, I am the happiest woman here today. That is because, as Beth's older sister, I know that she is being true to her heart, mind, and soul in marrying Brian. As a big sister, one who increasingly grew closer to Beth as we matured through the years, I had a unique vantage point into her life throughout our childhood and teenage years.

"Like all sisters, we experienced our normal roller coaster of good times and bad times together. These included our share of spats, particularly when we were younger. And just to clear up the record, I, not Beth, should have been punished for convincing her that if she removed Grandma's dentures from their soaking solution and left them on her nightstand overnight with a note to the tooth fairy, the tooth fairy would magically whiten the teeth and leave her with a quarter for each tooth in the morning. Keep in mind that a quarter was a lot of money to a little kid back in the day. This was just one of the many pranks I was able to pull off on my gullible baby sister.

"Beyond children just being children, Beth and I generally got along well, and we became close friends. I have always loved and enjoyed her sweet disposition and compassionate nature.

"From an early age, I knew that Beth had a penchant for taking care of others. During Beth's baby doll phase, she would treat Eric, her 'prematurely born' doll, as if he were an actual baby—wrapping him in a blanket, towing him around the house wherever she went, verifying that he was well, and 'teaching' him what to eat and how to behave.

"Shortly after Beth turned nine, she announced to our family that she wanted to dedicate her life to working as a medical professional. She made it clear that she wanted to do this not for money, prestige, or recognition but to fulfill our Christian mission of helping those in need, especially those who otherwise would not receive adequate medical treatment. This came days after the tragic death of a young black girl named Isoke, who bled to death while waiting for an ambulance in apartheid-era South Africa.

"This traumatic experience and the subsequent ten days we spent in Soweto ministering to the medical needs of poverty-stricken South Africans suffering from tuberculosis, diphtheria, and malaria forged Beth's resolve to undertake this noble mission.

"Since then, Beth has become an RN at Johns Hopkins and done a tremendous amount of charitable work to help fund medical research for AIDS, breast cancer, premature babies, cystic fibrosis, and Parkinson's disease. She has also continued to volunteer for medical mission trips around the world to assist those suffering from natural disasters, war, famine, and epidemics.

"Thus, it should come as no surprise to us today that Beth has chosen to spend the rest of her life with a likeminded man, who, besides being a great fiancée and friend, is dedicated to bettering the lives of those with medical needs on foreign battlefields and in hospitals here at home.

"Thank you for indulging me to share a few recollections and thoughts with you about my wonderful sister and best friend, Beth.

So, without further ado, I propose an old Irish toast to Beth and to Brian Johnson. 'May your neighbors respect you, trouble neglect you, the angels protect you, and heaven accept you.'"

"*Slainte!*" Eamon cried out, raising his glass in the traditional Gaelic toast, which translated, "To your health!"

"*Slainte!*" A few of the Irish old-timers from Beth's family echoed Eamon's response as the rest of the wedding guests raised their glasses in toast to the couple.

Stephen presently rose to give the blessing for the dinner that was about to be served. Before his father could utter a word, however, Brian stood and whispered to his father that he wished to address the gathering. A bit startled, Brian's father slowly nodded and took his seat.

Anxious with anticipation, Brian scanned the faces of his wedding guests. His heart pounding, he prepared to deliver the most difficult and courageous speech of his life.

CHAPTER 16

S tanding at the head of the wedding table, Brian gathered himself, cleared his throat and began.

"First of all, on behalf of Beth and me, I would like to thank each and every one of you for traveling here today to share this defining moment in our lives. Many of you, including my 'band of brothers' seated here among us, have sacrificed much to be here, utilizing precious time and traveling great distances at considerable expense to join us. You, our closest friends and family, have gathered here today to support and celebrate our marriage.

"Whether by blood or friendship, you are our family—the people whose love and support has shaped who we are and who we will be for the rest of our lives—and we will never forget that. No matter where we find ourselves in the future, we know that you will be with us, whether in person or in spirit.

"Today, we are blessed to be able to fellowship with all of you in person, and the singularity of this event is not lost on us. It is because of this, and the sad recognition that this may be my last opportunity to be with many of you, that I feel compelled to share with you an intensely personal journey—a journey that few among you realize I have commenced.

"One month and nine days ago, I learned that I have stage IV melanoma—skin cancer that has spread from my neck to my shoulders and left lung."

Brian could hear the sound of horrified gasps and sighs fill the air. From his peripheral vision, he could see faces tightening with grief and pain. Nonetheless, he pressed on, resolved and undeterred to share his message.

"I was told that unless my body responded well to an aggressive course of treatment, I might only have six to eight months to live," he continued, swallowing hard, as the initial round of sighs and gasps gave way to a palpable silence that hung in the air like a dense, suffocating fog.

"Three weeks ago, I began a combination drug therapy regimen. So that I would have the strength to participate in today's ceremony, I have thus far only undergone the first of six cycles of chemotherapy. At this stage, it is too early to judge the efficacy of the treatment. It may lead to complete remission of my cancer. It may prolong my life by slowing its spread or reducing the size of the tumors. Or it may fail altogether. There are other treatment options, such as radiotherapy and immunotherapy, that can be tried, but time may be short.

"Having said all this, your first reaction may be to feel sorry for me. But before you do, I want to let you know what I feel in my heart. Echoing the words of baseball legend Lou Gehrig, which are immortalized in his farewell address at Yankee Stadium, I say to you with profound gratitude, 'Today I consider myself the luckiest man on the face of the earth.'[5]

---

5   Lou Gehrig, Farewell to Baseball address, delivered July 4, 1939, Yankee Stadium, New York, published in American Rhetoric, Top 100 Speeches https://www.americanrhetoric.com/speeches/lougehrigfarewelltobaseball.htm.

"I do not, for a second, believe that I merit mention in the same breath as the iconic Hall of Famer, who is one of our most beloved sports heroes. However, to illustrate a point, please indulge me to mention a few words about him.

"Lou Gehrig was one of the most impactful baseball players of all time: a 1934 Triple Crown Champion and six-time World Series Champion, who set a record for playing in the most consecutive major league games that lasted for over half a century.

"After starting 2,130 consecutive games for the New York Yankees, Lou Gehrig displayed unimaginable courage and character when he removed himself from the lineup with the realization that he could no longer contribute to his team. Less than two months later, on his thirty-sixth birthday, he was diagnosed with an incurable neuromuscular disease called ALS—more commonly known today as Lou Gehrig's disease.

"Addressing his teammates and fans for the last time in his Yankee uniform, Gehrig called himself the 'luckiest man on the face of the earth.' Two years later, he departed us in body but not in spirit.

"I am standing before you today, but only God knows whether this will be my farewell address to some of you. But I want you to know that, like Lou Gehrig, I have received great love and support from my parents. I would like to acknowledge their being there for me time and again before all of you here today. I would also like to thank my beloved wife, Beth, for being my rock—my Gibraltar—who has enabled me to weather this storm . . ."

Brian saw that Beth had covered her face, and she appeared to be sobbing softly. He paused, struggling to maintain his composure.

God, please give me the strength to continue, he silently prayed. After a few moments, he cleared his throat and continued. "I'd like to share with all of you here today what a blessing Beth has been in my life by echoing some words from Gehrig's farewell address. 'When you have a wife who has been a tower of strength and shown more courage than you dreamed existed—that's the finest I know.'"[6]

"We love you Brian and Beth!" his father called out.

"We love you!" more and more guests shouted, rising to their feet.

With nearly every guest on their feet, the applause was thunderous, strengthening Brian's resolve to continue with strength and dignity.

After taking in a deep breath, Brian said, "You may be asking yourself why we chose to get married given this uncertainty overhanging my life. When I approached Beth following my diagnosis and asked her whether she wanted to reconsider our marriage in light of this, she told me that no matter what happened, I would be the love of her life. She went on to say that she wanted us to spend the rest of our lives together—no matter how long or short that might be. I have been unable to dissuade her from this position," Brian said with a touch of levity, gazing into Beth's tear-streaked eyes.

"I am at peace with whatever happens in my life, and it is important to me that you understand why. Before I begin, please understand that I am sharing my sincere thoughts with you and do not intend to preach to anyone here today. If I inadvertently cross over that line, please excuse me, given I am a youth pastor and the son of a Baptist pastor.

"First and foremost, my peace concerning my uncertain future rests in my strong and abiding faith that, following physical death

---

6   Ibid.

here on earth, I will experience a new and eternal life with Christ in a spiritual body that can never be broken or destroyed. That life will be an abundant one—more fulfilling than anything any of us could ever know or experience here on earth.

"Secondly, I have had the opportunity to see and do much in my life—more than I could have ever dreamed of doing. I have traveled on missionary trips to Kenya, Ethiopia, Bolivia, China, and Turkey, meeting my soulmate on my first medical mission trip to Kenya. Through a high school foreign exchange program, God afforded me the opportunity to study in Switzerland for a semester and to explore much of Europe: a wonderfully rich and diverse continent deeply steeped in history. My military service has likewise enabled me to travel to places I would not otherwise have ever had the opportunity to explore, including the ruggedly beautiful countries of Afghanistan and Uzbekistan. These travels have enabled me to make new friends on five different continents and to appreciate their fascinating cultures and ways of life.

"Thirdly, I have been blessed with the opportunity to help others. God has bestowed on me the means, skills, and disposition to assist those with medical needs, whether in a civilian or military role. He has given me a yearning to serve my country and introduced me to fellow soldiers—brothers and sisters—who have incalculably bettered my life through providing living examples of duty, loyalty, sacrifice, and love for country and their fellow man.

"It is with true sadness that I recognize today that it is unlikely that I will be able to return soon to serve alongside you. Just as Lou Gehrig sadly, but honestly, recognized in the spring of 1939, I realize at this point that I would be more of a liability than an asset in the field. But believe me, there is not one day that passes that I do not think of you and thank God for your service—"

"We love you, Brian!" John shouted out, rising to his feet, unable to maintain his silence.

The rest of his Ranger comrades likewise rose to their feet and shouted out, "We're here for you, Bri," and "You're our brother, forever."

A marine among them cried out, "Semper fi!"

Brian turned to them and saluted, fighting once again to keep his composure.

"Thank you; you're family to me," he managed to say. "I would like to take this opportunity to also recognize all the members of our armed forces, whether you are on active duty, in the reserves, or a veteran. Would each of you please stand?"

One by one, each past or present member of the U.S. Army, Navy, Air Force, Marines, and Coast Guard stood and received a sustained, heartfelt round of applause from the newlyweds, their parents, and everyone around them. Many rose to their feet, including an old man on crutches and an elderly woman battling Parkinson's disease. The sentiment, and the energy behind it, were palpable to all present.

"Thank you," Brian said at long last. As the applause slowed, he continued, "Perhaps this goes without saying, but the relationships I have been privileged to forge with each of you gives me strength. And my union this day with Beth—my best friend and soulmate—instills peace within me. My faith and the promises of Scripture nourish my soul with hope—hope for a good and abundant life, whether here on earth or in Heaven.

"Just as I was prepared to lay down my life for my brothers and my country in Afghanistan, I submit my life to God's will this evening.

I am ready to lose my life for His sake—should that be His will. That does not mean that with every ounce of my strength and every part of my will, I will not strive to defeat this cancer. Regardless of the outcome, however, I rest assured and am at peace, knowing that I will experience God's grace and mercy *either way*. No matter what God's plan, I am and will remain content that I have learned how to live a life full of love, joy, and sacrifice, founded on principles of honor, service, and integrity and rooted in the foundation of my faith."

Raising his glass for the last time before all those gathered there before him, Brian's voice rang out with clarity, inspiring them with a toast they would never forget. "My friends and family, I say to you today, rejoice with me, for I have lived!"

EPILOGUE

An orb of light in human form stood silently before the gates of a radiant city as clear as crystal and more brilliant than the sun, towered by bejeweled walls. Jasper, sapphire, agate, emerald, onyx, carnelian, and other jewels of sparkling purity dazzled in unblemished light.

The being gazed beyond a gate formed from a single pearl, resplendent in its iridescent beauty. Before him stretched streets of gold and a river of crystal flowing toward a magnificent throne upon which a glorious Ruler sat, gleaming from head to toe. Ushered into the Ruler's presence by a beautiful angel, the being fell to his knees, faint of heart and strength—completely awestruck. The being dared not gaze up at a King as luminous as lightning, Whose eyes burned with holy flame.

Presently, a voice as gentle as a shepherd's and as deep as the ocean communicated without speech, "Rise, Brian, my son, for your name is written in the Book of Life. I welcome you, my good and faithful servant, to My Kingdom."

Rising to his feet, the overcome being answered, "Praise be to You, my Lord and Savior for eternity! Though Heaven and earth may pass, Your glory will never depart. I am utterly unworthy to stand here in Your presence."

"All are unworthy" rumbled like ocean waves through Brian's being. "Your faith in the Lamb has freed you of all that is unworthy, and I have answered your prayers for forgiveness, just as you forgave the transgressions of those who wronged you. Strengthened by your faith in my Son, you loved Me as a son loves a father with the strength of your heart, mind, and soul. Furthermore, each time you sacrificed in love for others and helped heal and restore even the least of your brethren on earth, you demonstrated your love for Me. Willing to lay down your life for others, you embodied the words of my Son, 'Greater love has no one than this, that someone lay down his life for his friends.'"[7]

"My Lord and my God," Brian's being responded, moved most powerfully to bow in reverence.

"Moreover, throughout your life, you honored your father, Stephen, and your mother, Catherine. Thus, I honored you with a long life upon the earth."

"Glory to You, my Savior and King! Your blessings and mercy are beyond comprehension. When I completely yielded my life to You, You healed me. Then with great compassion, You blessed Beth and me with precious gifts: a twin son and daughter—Caleb and Rebecca—beautiful, healthy children created in Your image. Our hearts can never repay Your goodness and generosity. May Your name forever be praised!"

"Rest assured, one day, they, too, and your beloved wife, will join you and your parents here, for each of their names are also written in the Book of Life. Now, rise, My child, for your robes have been washed clean in the holy blood of My Son, the life-giving Lamb!"

---

7   John 15:13

Gesturing to a tree with leaves that never wither but glisten in golden radiance on either side of the river, the dazzling King invited Brian to partake. "Come and eat from one of the twelve fruits of the tree of life, upon which you and your family will feast in My Kingdom for eternity."

Greeted in the purest and most refreshing embrace he had ever experienced from his loving parents, Brian proceeded with them, heavenly hand in hand. Toward the tree of life they walked, as one family, bonded by joy beyond comprehension and eager to be nourished by healing fruit in their Father's glorious Kingdom for all eternity.

For more information about
Douglas J. Lanzo
and
I Have Lived
please visit:

www.douglaslanzo.com

Ambassador International's mission is to magnify the Lord Jesus Christ
and promote His Gospel through the written word.

We believe through the publication of Christian literature, Jesus Christ and
His Word will be exalted, believers will be strengthened in their walk with
Him, and the lost will be directed to Jesus Christ as the only way of salvation.

For more information about
AMBASSADOR INTERNATIONAL
please visit:

www.ambassador-international.com

*Thank you for reading this book. Please consider leaving us a
review on your social media, favorite retailer's website,
Goodreads or Bookbub, or our website.*

If it's true that "all comic novels must be about matters of life and death," *The Honest Atheist* obliges. This entertaining and thought-provoking tragicomedy provides clues to where our loss of public decency originates while telling a moving story of an unlikely friendship between an atheist and an evangelical Christian.

Charlotte Hallaway needs to come to terms with her father's death. He had been her only family, and she wasn't handling her grief well. It was just supposed to be a few weeks of peace and quiet to process it all, but then she saw them—a drug deal and a murder within seconds of each other. And they saw her. Now running for her life, Charlotte boards a bus to escape her pursuers and wakes up the next morning in the woods without a memory of how she got there or of who she is.

Betty is sure that Ida Lou does not belong in their church when the woman shows up to the Good Friday service with her small dog in tow. But before she knows what's happening, Betty—along with the other women of the WUFHs (Women United For Him)—is pushed into helping the woman. God works in mysterious ways—and through ordinary people. The town of Prosper is about to experience some drama—and it all starts with a dog who comes to church.

www.ingramcontent.com/pod-product-compliance
Lightning Source LLC
Chambersburg PA
CBHW071957170626
46813CB00005B/1908